DOM

HELL SQUAD #18

ANNA HACKETT

Dom

Published by Anna Hackett

Copyright 2019 by Anna Hackett

Cover by Melody Simmons of BookCoversCre8tive

Edits by Tanya Saari

ISBN (ebook): 978-1-925539-74-5

ISBN (paperback): 978-1-925539-75-2

Beneath a Trojan Moon – SFR Galaxy Award Winner and RWAus Ella Award Winner

Hell Squad – SFR Galaxy Award for best Post-Apocalypse for Readers who don't like Post-Apocalypse

The Anomaly Series – #1 Amazon Action Adventure Romance Bestseller

"Like Indiana Jones meets Star Wars. A treasure hunt with a steamy romance." – SFF Dragon, review of *Among Galactic Ruins*

"Strap in, enjoy the heat of romance and the daring of this group of space travellers!" – Di, Top 500 Amazon Reviewer, review of *At Star's End*

"Action, danger, aliens, romance – yup, it's another great book from Anna Hackett!" – Book Gannet Reviews, review of *Hell Squad: Marcus*

Sign up for my VIP mailing list and get your *free box set* containing three action-packed romances.

Visit here to get started:
www.annahackettbooks.com

CHAPTER ONE

S he shouldn't be out here.

Arden had snuck out of the Enclave again. While she was beyond grateful for the safety of the secret underground base she called home, sometimes she needed to breathe. Sometimes, she needed a break from the walls around her.

She lifted her face to the sky and took a deep breath. The Enclave provided safety and security, and protected the human survivors from the alien invaders. The reptilian Gizzida had come two years ago, and ripped the world apart.

Torn families apart.

Arden's belly clenched. The aliens had killed friends, lovers, parents, husbands, and children. She had quickly learned that grief had very sharp claws.

In the early days, after she'd lost her husband and kids, she'd been shredded inside, but now, she didn't bleed quite as much.

She stared at the sunset. The sun was sinking down beyond the western horizon, turning the sky shades of gold streaked with pink. She sighed at the beauty. She could see the beauty now. For so long, the world around her had been nothing but dreary shades of gray.

But now she could smile at the sunset, and remember the family she'd lost without ending up curling into a ball and weeping.

I miss you, guys.

Jason, her husband, had been a high school principal. A lanky, easygoing man with a mop of sandy-colored hair, he'd been dedicated to his job. He'd loved his school, loved his wife, and adored his family.

Her kids. Arden bit down on her bottom lip. Elisabeth—call me Beth—had been eleven going on twenty. Emmett had been her sweet, kind seven-year-old boy who'd loved soccer and drawing.

Letting the emotions flow inside her, Arden pulled out her sketchbook. She lifted her charcoal and quickly started sketching the sunset. Behind her, the eastern horizon grew darker, and night started to sweep across the sky.

The Enclave was near Wollongong, just south of Sydney, Australia. The area consisted of rolling, green fields, and small towns that had at one time thrived from the constant buzz of nearby Sydney—once the capital of the United Coalition of Countries. Now, this place was home to the survivors, and the squads fighting back for humanity's survival. And most of the time, everyone stayed safe and secure, deep within the Enclave.

With the exception of a couple of the survivors, like Arden, who had tricks up their sleeves for sneaking out.

The reason she could sneak out so easily was that she was a comms officer for Squad Nine. She smiled to herself. She'd never imagined she'd put her office-manager skills to use providing comms and intel to a tough squad of soldiers fighting against aliens, but here she was.

She was good at her job. Not only that, being a comms officer had helped her through her grief, kept her sane. And because of it, she knew all the camera locations around the base, and the patrol schedules. It made it easy for her to slip in and out when she needed some air.

She dragged in another deep breath and tipped her face up to watch the stars appearing in the sky. Just a few more minutes and she'd go back inside.

"I warned you about coming out here."

The deep voice made her freeze. It held a touch of a sexy Italian accent.

She turned slowly, her belly quivering and her skin prickling.

Dominic Santora was the definition of dark, lean, and lethal. He had thick, black hair with a hint of curl, dark eyes, sharp cheekbones, and skin a glorious shade of bronze. He radiated a dangerous intensity that often made people take a step back when they encountered him.

He was scowling at her.

"It's dangerous for you to be outside the base," he said.

Arden straightened. "I know."

He was wearing his black, carbon-fiber armor, his carbine slung over his shoulder. He stepped closer and she smelled him. She was pretty sure he wore some sort of cologne. Her gaze slipped down his lean, muscled body. She'd never thought she'd find carbon fiber sexy.

"You have a death wish?" he growled.

She sucked in a breath. "No."

"I warned you the last time I caught you out here. If a raptor gets close enough, they'll snatch you quicker than you can blink. Or if some canid jumps on you, it'll tear that soft skin of yours to shreds."

She stared into his dark eyes and her brain went blank. Reflected in the darkness of his gaze, she saw that he was a man who'd seen way too much in his life.

And not just the death, blood, and destruction of the Gizzida invasion, but in his life before that.

She'd heard the whispers. That Dom had once worked for the Mafia in Italy.

"Come on." He grabbed her arm.

As soon as he touched her, electricity snapped between them. She gasped and he cursed. His fingers flexed around her bicep. He was wearing gloves and, for a second, she wished he wasn't.

Then he tugged her toward the closest entrance back into the base. As she moved, her sketchbook fell from her hand. Darn, she'd forgotten about it. It landed on the grass, opening on the page she'd been working on, with her sunset picture.

Dom went down on one knee and picked up the book. He studied it. "This is good."

"Thank you." She rarely showed anyone her work.

She'd drawn as a child before she'd given it up for "real" work. It was only recently that she'd started doodling and taking some art classes. She reached for the book, but he held it away from her.

Her heart started pounding. "Don't—"

He flipped the page.

Oh, God. She felt heat wash over her skin. The next page showed a sketch of him.

His face was in profile, the hard lines of it etched on the page. He stared at it for a moment before he turned the page again.

Another one of him. In this one, he was in his armor, his hands on his lean hips. She'd done it from memory, from one of the numerous times that she'd seen them in the Hawk quadcopter hangar, getting prepped for a mission.

Arden licked her lips and wondered if the ground could just open up and swallow her whole. When she looked up, that dark gaze was resting on her face.

She waited for him to say something. To *do* something.

Sensations danced in her belly. She realized she *wanted* him to do something. She swallowed, and wondered how she could feel so desperate, excited, and afraid all at the same time.

Then Dom snapped the sketchbook closed and handed it back to her. "You have talent."

He reached for her arm again and pulled her toward the hidden Enclave entrance.

Blinking, Arden stumbled. Thankfully, he steadied her.

That was it? He'd seen that she'd been sort-of stalking him, drawing pictures of him, and he had nothing to say about it?

He paused beside a group of trees, and touched a hidden keypad. The secret entrance to the base opened in the ground below.

He nodded his head. "Get inside."

She walked down the steps and into the base. Of course, that was it. Dom was part of Squad Three—the wild, bad-boy soldiers known as the berserkers. Several of them had recently fallen in love and found partners, but there were plenty of stories about the berserkers. They could have their pick of any willing, gorgeous female in the Enclave. Arden had overheard plenty of sigh-filled stories of wild, sexy nights.

Why would anyone want an almost-forty-year-old, uninteresting woman like her?

"Arden?"

She looked up at him. He stood above her, the night casting him in shadows. If it was possible, he looked even more dark and dangerous than usual.

"I warned you once, and this makes twice. I catch you out here again, there will be consequences." His deep, liquid voice rolled over her.

Then, a second later, the door closed between them.

Arden blew out a breath.

She stood there, staring at the heavy-metal door. *What was wrong with her?* She pressed her hand to her flushed face. This was crazy.

Because she suddenly realized that she *wanted* consequences.

She was finally shaking off the worst of her grief, only to find herself hopelessly attracted to a dark, deadly man. And she had no idea what to do about it.

FINISHED WITH PATROL, Dom headed down the Enclave corridor, his carbine over his shoulder. He was due to meet his squad in the Command Center.

He turned into another corridor and heard the noise from the dining room ahead. It was dinner time, so the place was packed. Survivors were in there, eating their meals, talking, connecting.

As he moved past the doors, without realizing, he scanned the crowd, searching for one slender figure with porcelain skin, light-brown hair, and eyes of such a pretty blue they looked violet.

Sei un idiota. He swung his head to look straight ahead and kept walking.

Arden Erica Carlisle was *not* for him.

She was beauty, grace, kindness. He ground his teeth together. He wouldn't sully her with his darkness.

He approached the Command Center, the glass doors whispering open. Staff members were busy at the tiers of computers. A large screen dominated the main wall. As he stepped inside, he spotted his squad. They were a rough bunch. Most of the squads were made up of soldiers and former law enforcement.

Squad Three, however, was made up of former mercenaries, bikers, and criminals. A smile tugged at his lips. They were the wildest squad in the base, but they knew how to fight.

As he approached, the guys lifted their hands and called out hellos. At the front of the room stood Niko Ivanov, the civilian leader of the Enclave, and General Adam Holmes, the man in charge of the military and security side of things. The general nodded at him.

Dom felt a weird throb under his ribs. It happened all the time. He was *welcome* here. He'd never truly belonged anywhere before, and had either been ignored or eyed warily. But at the Enclave, his squad mates were now his friends, and he was respected by the general and Niko.

In his previous life, he'd attended plenty of high-powered meetings. He'd witnessed more Mafia power games, standing at Salvatore Denaro's side, than he liked to remember. The man had been the ruthless head of the Ndrangheta.

And Dom had been his enforcer, his bogeyman used to scare Salvatore's rivals. Salvatore's personal killer.

Shaking off the memories, Dom joined his squad. But even as he pushed the memories away, he still felt the darkness clinging to him like filth.

Holmes stepped forward to address the squads. "The tracker on the Gizzida bomb is still functioning. It's moving slowly north."

On a previous mission into the mountains, Dom's squad had located the mysterious octagon bomb the aliens had created. No one knew exactly what chaos it could cause, but they'd managed to get a tracker on it.

"They haven't found the tracker?" Marcus Steele, leader of Hell Squad asked.

"It appears that they haven't," the general said.

Niko frowned. "Although if they have, they could be leaving the tracker active in order to set a trap for us."

"A risk we'll have to take." The general's piercing blue eyes scanned the room. "Once the bomb stops moving, the plan is to send in some squads to investigate. Squad Three, you're on standby for the mission. Squad Nine will be back up."

"Bring it on." Hemi Rahia pumped a fist into the air. The bearded berserker was always ready for a fight.

Dom saw their squad leader and Hemi's brother, Tane, lift his chin. Today, his dark dreadlocks were pulled back from his face. He had dark-bronze skin like Dom, but his was thanks to his Maori heritage. The former mercenary was a hell of a fighter and a good leader.

When the meeting broke up, Dom followed his squad to the gym.

His friend, Griff, fell into step beside him. "How was patrol? Boring?"

"Yeah." Dom's thoughts instantly veered to Arden.

Griff smiled. "I don't know why you always volunteer for extra patrol shifts." The former cop and ex-con shook his head. "While you were out there, my woman nabbed me." Griff grinned widely. "I got lucky."

Dom studied the man and noted the lipstick on his collar. No guesses needed to work out what Griff and Indy had been up to. Indy was the wild, bold comms officer for their squad. After dancing around each other for quite some time, Griff was now happily besotted with his woman.

It was good. Dom was happy for his friend. After everything he'd been through, Griff deserved some good in his life.

They reached the gym, and while the others started working out, Dom headed into their squad locker room. He stripped the rest of his gear off and stowed it in his locker.

In the men's room, he washed up. As he looked himself over in the mirror on the wall, he thought of Arden's sketches of him.

She'd been drawing him. He pressed his hands to the edge of the sink and sucked in a breath. That meant she'd been thinking about him.

What he'd seen in those pictures... His fingers curled around the cool porcelain. She hadn't drawn him looking scary or evil. She'd drawn him looking thoughtful, heroic.

He stared into the mirror. She clearly had a good imagination.

He glanced at the black ink resting on his hip. It was in Italian—*vivere liberamente*. Live freely. The words were a harsh reminder to himself that he was never free.

Back at his locker, Dom pulled on his workout gear, then headed back into the gym.

The others were spread out—Levi and Ash running on the treadmills, Hemi and Griff lifting weights, and Tane kickboxing with one of the heavy-duty bags hanging from the ceiling. Dom headed over to join Tane.

"So," Hemi called out, "with Griff all loved up with

Indy, that means we need to find Dom and Tane some women."

Tane ignored his brother, landing a hard kick to the bag. The chain rattled.

Dom lifted his fists and landed a few hard jabs to the canvas. He never used gloves.

"Let's see," Hemi mused. "Maybe some pretty blonde for Dom?"

"I like brunettes." *Cazzo*, why had he said that?

"A-ha." Hemi pointed at him. "Then we'll find you a pretty brunette, my man." Hemi looked at his brother. "And I think my bro seems to have a preference for silver hair."

Tane kicked the bag so hard that it fell off the chain and landed on the floor. "Shut it, Hemi."

Hemi was shorter than his brother, but broader. He didn't seem intimidated by Tane's sharp tone. "Why would I want to do that?"

Dom knew the silver reference was to Selena—the alien woman and ally who now lived at the Enclave. Hell Squad had rescued her from the Gizzida months before. When she'd first arrived, she'd been a shell-shocked kidnap survivor. But lately, she'd been coming into her own strength.

And she was powerful as hell.

"I hear the doc's running more tests on Selena," Ash said.

Tane's head jerked up. "Tests? She's been through enough."

"She has skills and abilities that can help us fight the Gizzida," Levi said.

Hemi nodded. "Yeah, without her, there's no way we'd have gotten away on that last mission in Katoomba."

Dom's gut tightened. Without Selena, Griff would've died on that mission. The alien woman had the ability to tap into the planet's natural energy. She could connect with animals, and hell, he'd seen her control the very ground under their feet.

"She isn't a fucking weapon." Tane snatched up a towel, wiping his face. Then he tossed it in the bin near the door. "I've got things to do." He strode out of the gym.

Hemi just shook his head, watching the empty doorway. "Okay, who wants to place bets on how long it takes my little bro to stake a claim on our resident alien?"

"I'm in," Levi called.

Griff nodded. "Me, too."

Dom ignored them, turning back to his punching bag. His friends were so blissed up from being in love, they wanted the same for everyone else. He thought briefly of Arden, then blocked her out of his head.

He pounded the bag until his arms ached.

CHAPTER TWO

"Okay, step to the left."

Arden did as instructed, and as she moved, the high-tech drone hovering over her left shoulder moved with her. She laughed. "This is amazing, Noah."

The head of the tech team nodded, his long, dark hair moving around his hawkish face. A small smile flirted around his mouth.

He didn't need her to tell him it was amazing. He was a genius, and he knew it. They were in his tech lab in the heart of the Enclave. The room was packed with desks loaded with comp parts, wires, and, well, a bunch of stuff she didn't recognize. Behind Noah was a shelf, and lined up on it was the man's prized dice collection. No one was allowed to touch them.

The rest of his tech team were out in other parts of the base, keeping the Enclave's systems running, the lights on, and the soldiers in weapons. In addition to keeping his team on their toes, Noah still had time to work on new devices, like this combat drone.

Arden watched as the drone hovered above her. Noah had needed a guinea pig to help him test the drone and Arden had volunteered. Unlike others in the base, who had partners or children, she didn't. And lately, her best friend Indy was busy sneaking off to have sex with Griff at every opportunity.

That left Arden with plenty of free time.

She touched the back of her hand, her fingers running over the light bump of the chip under her skin. Noah had implanted the computer chip that linked her to the new combat drone a few weeks before.

It wasn't like any of the normal drones that the drone team used for surveillance and intel—this one was larger, had pinchers at the front for grabbing things, and its rotors were encased below its main body.

Noah leaned against his desk. "Okay, move around the lab. Let's test the targeting."

Arden circled the desks and chairs. The drone followed her.

Noah nodded, his gaze narrowed.

"Target." She pointed at a chair.

The drone spun, it's laser weapons swiveling to aim at the chair.

This drone was also equipped with weapons. *Wow*. It was pretty cool.

Noah nodded. "The chip has integrated well. It's tied into your nervous system and I'm really happy with the results."

"Target doorway." At the sound of her voice, the drone swiveled.

Arden smiled, feeling more than a little badass. Her squad had four badass female soldiers, and for a second, she felt like one of the team.

"Noah...oh, sorry to interrupt."

The feminine voice came from the doorway. Arden glanced over her shoulder and saw Selena. The woman's silver-white hair was pulled back in a ponytail. Resting on her shoulder was a giant black bird.

The bird took one look at the drone, squawked, then attacked in a flurry of fluttering wings.

Oh, crap. Arden panicked, leaping back, and ramming into a chair. Her drone, sensing her fright, moved in front of her. Protecting her.

Its lasers swiveled to lock onto the bird. Noah cursed, and as the bird's claws slashed out, the drone dodged to the side. Lasers fired, blasts singeing the wall.

Arden swallowed a cry and ducked down. "Drone, disengage. Disengage."

"Fluffy, no." Selena threw out a slim hand.

Energy filled the room, and Fluffy froze midair. The alien hybrid bird hovered there, wings fluttering. Then the gyr flew back to Selena, landing on her outstretched arm.

Arden slowly rose. She'd heard about Selena's abilities. The woman, like all her species, was connected to nature. Selena could tap into natural energy and even command animals. It was mind-boggling.

"I'm so sorry, Noah," Selena said. "I didn't realize you had a drone in here."

"It's fine, Selena. You're here for this?" He held out a flat, portable comp from his desk. "It's all fixed."

"Thank you." Selena took the tablet, her overlarge green eyes warm. "I've become a little addicted to some of the shows in the base database. I've been missing them since Fluffy cracked the screen."

"Any time," Noah said.

"Sorry, Arden." Selena sent Arden a shy smile. "Fluffy still forgets drones aren't the enemy."

"It's fine. No harm."

With a nod, Selena left. Arden straightened, admiring the confidence in the woman's steps. She'd come so far since her rescue.

So many of them had. From those terrible, horrifying early days of the invasion, they'd found some semblance of normality.

But Arden knew that the Gizzida would keep hunting them. A cold shiver hit her. The aliens wanted Earth and its resources. They would eventually hunt down all the survivors.

Unless the humans found a way to stop them.

Noah reached up and powered down the drone. He set it down on the bench. "I think that's enough for today. Thanks for your help with this."

She nodded. "I'm happy to help."

He gave her a chin lift. "Same time tomorrow? We might head into a larger space and test some new features."

"It's a date," she said.

"Hope you aren't making dates with other women."

The voice made Arden swivel to see the redhead standing in the doorway.

"Hey there, Captain Dragon," Noah drawled.

Arden watched Noah's stern face light up. Laura Bladon, head of the interrogation team, smiled back at her man. The woman took two steps into the room before Noah was on her, sweeping her into his arms.

Watching the couple kiss made something move through Arden. She felt the love pulsing off them.

Once, Arden had been loved like that.

While Noah and Laura were lost in each other, she snuck out of the lab.

Heading down the corridor, she wrapped her arms around her middle. She missed that. That sense of belonging. She missed sex. She missed snuggling on the couch. She missed sharing a glass of wine with someone.

And she missed her kids.

Hot tears pricked at her eyes. She missed sweet cuddles, messy rooms, toys underfoot, little kids' laughter.

She missed it all, but she wouldn't let herself cry for Jason, Beth, and Emmett anymore. Now, she tried to honor them by remembering the good times. She knew in her heart that they wouldn't want her to be so sad. She'd shed so many tears over the last couple of years, and she knew that her hubby and kids would hate to know that she'd been so lost and alone.

Suddenly, Arden's chest was so tight that she couldn't breathe.

Air. She needed air.

She broke into a run, sprinting into another corridor. She

rushed past a group of residents, heading for the closest exit. The tie in her hair slipped loose, her hair spilling around her shoulders. She reached the door, overrode the locking mechanism, and without stopping to think, shoved the door open.

Arden rushed into the darkness, running through the thick grass and into the field above the Enclave.

When she stopped, she was panting, but thankfully the pain had dulled.

Pressing her palms to her eyes, it almost hurt to realize that what she felt wasn't the piercing, shattering grief that had once gutted her. Now, it was just a dull throb. A sad reminder that something she loved was missing.

She stood there, lifting her gaze to the stars in the inky sky above. She dragged in some deep breaths, waiting for her pulse rate to calm.

Then she heard a rustle.

A chill skated over her and she went still. Dom's warnings rattled in her head.

No. There was no way that raptors were this close to the Enclave. There were soldiers on patrol, drones flying overhead, security cameras.

She strained to listen but heard nothing but the wind ruffling her hair. She took a step back. She should go back inside.

But before she could move, a shadow detached from the ground, flowing upward.

Arden's throat closed.

The creature rose up in front of her.

It was covered in pitch-black scales. Her heart pounding in her ears, she watched it morph into a slender raptor, no taller than herself. Its body was lean and wiry, built for stealth, not power, like the regular raptor soldiers.

Suddenly, one sinewy arm flashed out and grabbed Arden's bicep. Its claws bit into her skin.

She tried to wrench away, but it was too strong. Its other arm grabbed her, and it lifted her off her feet.

Arden screamed.

DOM'S BOOTS crunched on the dirt. It had been a quiet evening on patrol. Beside him, Levi was cradling his carbine and eyeing the surrounding trees.

"You got plans after we finish?" Levi asked.

Dom shook his head. "You?"

"Gonna track down my woman. No doubt she'll be in the maintenance hangar, working on a vehicle." Levi's teeth flashed white in the darkness. "She looks pretty cute streaked with grease."

Chrissy usually worked on the Z6-Hunters, the armored vehicles the squads used in the field.

"No doubt," Dom replied. "She works hard."

Levi nodded. "I'll offer to scrub her back." He grinned again.

Dom grunted. It was fifty-fifty what Chrissy's reaction might be. The redhead lived up to the reputation, and had swung a wrench at Levi's head more than once.

Suddenly, a woman's scream pierced the night.

"What the fuck?" Levi barked.

Both of them broke into a run.

They rounded a small clump of trees in the field, and the scream sounded again. Levi and Dom whipped their carbines up, slowing down and moving forward cautiously.

Then Dom saw it.

The raptor was black, sinewy, and unlike any alien he'd seen yet. The creature was holding a struggling woman in its arms.

Dom's gut turned to rock. It was Arden.

"Let her go!" he yelled.

Arden turned her head, and in the moonlight, he saw her face was lined with fear. Her violet-blue gaze met his, and he saw a flash of relief.

The raptor made a grunting sound, turned, and started running through the long grass. It threw Arden over one lean shoulder.

Cursing, Dom and Levi gave chase, charging through the grass.

"We have some sort of stealth raptor out here," Levi barked into his earpiece. "It's got Arden."

"What?" Indy's voice came over the line. "Did you say Arden?"

"Yes," Dom replied. "We need backup, Indy. Now." He leaped over an uneven patch of ground.

The stealth raptor was damn fast. Dom sucked in air, pushing for more speed.

"This raptor is smaller, leaner, and faster," Levi said. "Covered in black, scaly skin."

"Okay, okay. I'm on it." Indy's voice was shaky. "Get her back, you guys."

"I can't get a shot," Levi said.

Dom couldn't either. There was too much risk of hitting Arden. He watched her twist around, ramming her elbow against the raptor's head.

The alien stumbled, then regained its balance. It gripped the back of her shirt and shook her so violently that her head flipped forward and back.

Cazzo. Dom dropped his carbine and yanked out his knives. "Keep him busy."

Levi nodded, firing into the night. The raptor skidded and spun. Arden had gone limp in his arms.

Be okay, bella. Dom crept up behind the raptor. The alien was focused on Levi, and Dom used the darkness to hide his approach. The dark was his old friend.

Just a bit closer. A bit closer. Dom leaped forward and jabbed the knife into the alien's lower back. The scales weren't as thick as a regular raptor's, the blade meeting little resistance.

The stealth raptor roared and spun.

Dom dropped low, slashing at the raptor's thigh.

As the creature roared again, Dom dodged and leaped up. He rammed his second blade into the alien's shoulder.

The raptor tripped, falling to the ground, trapping Arden beneath him.

Cursing, Dom dropped down. "Arden?"

"Dom!" she cried.

"Hang on, *bella.*"

Terrified eyes looked up into his. He yanked another knife off his belt and plunged it into the raptor's neck. The alien jerked and Dom slashed again, and again.

Blood spurted, and a second later, the raptor slumped and stopped moving.

Arden whimpered. "Get it off me!"

Dom gripped the creature and heaved it off her.

She sat up, shoving her hair out of her face.

"Jesus. Fuck." Levi appeared, keeping his carbine aimed at the raptor. He toed the creature. "Arden, you okay?"

Dom stayed crouched on one knee, watching her. She was panting, trying to pull herself together.

More than anything, he wanted to touch her. Instead, he curled his fingers into his palms. She was splattered with blood—red staining her face and clothes.

"I... I..."

"Take your time, darling," Levi said softly.

In the distance, shouts sounded. Their backup was coming.

Arden turned her head, her eyes meeting Dom's. They were wide and shocked.

He cleared his throat. She'd just watched him slaughter an alien and cover her in blood. She had a right to be afraid.

She launched herself at him.

Cazzo. He closed his arms around her. She pressed close, burying her face in his neck. She was shaking violently.

"I've got you," he murmured.

"Dom—" Her voice hitched.

He held her tighter. "You're safe now."

CHAPTER THREE

A rden couldn't slow her breathing. Her heart was pounding a hundred miles a minute, making her ribs ache.

Dom scooped her up off the ground.

Blood. There was so much blood. God, it was everywhere. Instantly, her mind plunged back to old memories, of the first wave of the invasion.

She lifted her head and saw Hell Squad rushing toward them.

Marcus Steele was in the lead. The big man's scarred face was serious as he scanned her and the dead raptor. Beside him stood his second, Cruz, with the rest of the squad fanned out behind them, all holding their weapons.

"Arden? You okay?" She recognized Shaw's easygoing drawl, although at this moment, it was filled with tension.

She looked at the sniper and managed a nod. Then she tucked her face back into Dom's neck and held on.

"I'll get her inside." Dom's deep voice rumbled beneath her ear. "She's not injured."

"We need the body." Marcus' gravelly drawl. "We need to get it to Doc Emerson so she can autopsy it."

"What the fuck is that?" The faint accent told her that it was Cruz speaking.

"It flowed up from the ground," Arden choked out. "Out of nowhere, like a shadow."

Dom's arms tightened around her, then he turned and walked away. Moments later, he was ducking inside the Enclave.

"We need to get the doc to check you over—"

Arden shook her head. "No. I'm not hurt. Please, I need to get clean. Please." She felt panic rising in her chest.

Dom was quiet for a beat. "Arden—"

"Please, Dom." She lifted her head and met his dark gaze. "When my family was killed—" her chest hitched "—I was covered in their blood."

He cursed softly in Italian. "Okay, *bella*. Hold on."

She did as told, holding onto him tightly. He was all hard-packed muscle, and the warmth of him helped her control the panic twisting in her belly. Soon, they reached her quarters. She didn't ask him how he knew where she lived. He shifted her so she could press her palm to the electronic lock.

He strode straight through her living area and into the bathroom. He set her down, and for a second, Arden wasn't sure her legs would hold her. But she locked her knees, determined to find some strength. She didn't want him to see her fall completely apart.

Then he dropped to his knees. Arden sucked in a breath, staring at his dark hair. He unlaced her shoes and pulled them off, one at a time. Her socks followed. He rose and started to undo the buttons on her shirt.

Arden just stood there and let him methodically strip her down to her underwear.

When he shifted away, she looked in the mirror and bile rose in her throat. Raptor blood was all over her skin.

Dom flicked on the tap and wet a cloth under the water. When he turned back to her, she realized she was shaking. He started wiping her face and neck.

"You've got this, Arden." His voice was quiet as he wiped across her collarbones, cleaning the blood away. "You held it together out there."

She looked up, and over his shoulder she saw their reflection. He was all darkness—dark hair, black armor—contrasting against her pale skin.

"There." He straightened.

The blood was gone. Arden stood there in her simple cotton underwear.

He turned to the sink, rinsing the cloth off.

"We were out for dinner in Sydney with the kids when the invasion happened." Her voice echoed off the tiles.

Dom went still and looked up. Their gazes met in the mirror.

"A ptero flew over the street where we were. There were explosions, screams." She swallowed. "The restaurant exploded. Jason, my husband, died instantly. My kids were hurt. I was hurt. I had burns on my arms and legs, and glass had hit me." She sucked in a shaky breath. "I was trapped under some rubble."

Dom turned. *"Bella—"*

She grabbed his hand, holding it like a lifeline.

"My daughter died first." Tears welled in Arden's eyes. "There wasn't time for Beth to be afraid. I held her hand."

Dom's fingers clenched on hers.

"I managed to get free and crawl to Emmett. He was still alive, but I could hear the rattle in his breathing. He was afraid." A tear slid down her cheek. "I held my son as he faded. I sang to him as he died."

With a muttered curse, Dom yanked her close. She burrowed into his chest, holding on to his strength.

"I'm so sorry, Arden." He smoothed a hand down her back.

"Me too." She let out a shuddering breath. "I shouldn't have been outside the Enclave."

"No, you shouldn't have."

She looked up at him. "You saved me."

"I killed in front of you, and covered you in blood." His voice was flat and held an edge.

She tilted her head, looking at his blank face. "If you hadn't killed that raptor, I'd be dead, or worse."

"I never wanted you to see that."

"I'm a comms officer. I see soldiers kill every day, Dom. Maybe not in real life, but I watch it on the feed. I direct my squad to the raptors to kill them. It's them or us, we all know that. You're a hero for protecting me and the other survivors, not a killer."

His dark eyes just stared at her, boiling with shadows. "I've always been a killer."

Arden swallowed. "You worked for the Mafia."

A short nod.

She was trying to find the right words to tell him that none of them were who they'd been before, but before she could, her legs gave way.

Dom caught her. He lifted her and carried her back into the other room. He gently set her on the bed, then grabbed the robe she'd left draped over the end of the bed. He wrapped it around her.

Suddenly, Arden was unbearably tired.

"Lie down." He nudged her back against the pillows.

"I..." She dropped back, fighting to keep her eyelids open.

"Adrenaline crash," he said.

There was a knock at the door. Eyeing her for a second, Dom touched her shoulder, then headed to answer the door. She heard him talking, then a woman's voice. *Indy*.

"She's fine," Dom said. "Falling asleep."

Arden let her eyes drift closed and the murmurs washed over her.

Then she heard someone moving beside the bed. When she opened her eyes, she saw Dom was back. He dimmed the lights and leaned over her.

"Sleep, *bella*." A brush of lips at her hairline.

When he drew back, she reached out and grabbed his arm. "Don't go."

Silence. "What do you need, Arden?"

"Don't leave me. I couldn't bear to be alone."

More silence, then she heard rustling. She realized he was taking off his carbon fiber armor. She heard water running in the bathroom.

A moment later, he climbed onto the bed, pulling her to his side.

She pressed her face to a chest that was now covered in a soft T-shirt. She sighed, her muscles relaxing.

For the first time in a very long time, Arden felt completely safe.

She let sleep drag her under.

DARKNESS CLUNG to him like tar. Dom tried to fling it away, but it crawled over him, smothering him.

He knew he was dreaming. This nightmare was his constant companion. The black turned to blood, covering his skin, soaking his hair.

You're nothing, Dominic. Salvatore's voice. *You're the son of a whore. A killer. Unwanted. Nothing.*

"Dom. Dom."

He felt soft hands on his face.

Dom jerked awake. He blinked and Arden's concerned face came into view.

For a moment, he was confused. Then he realized he was in Arden's bed, and she was pressed against him, her slender body covered only by her underwear, and a very thin layer of dark-green silk.

Her scent—delicate, floral—washed over him. He managed to shake off the remnants of the dream.

She'd been through a tough time. And then she'd

relived the attack that had taken her family. Now, he'd brought more darkness into her bed.

He sat up, throwing his legs over the edge of the bed.

"No." She grabbed his shoulders.

"I need to go."

"I don't want you to go."

He looked at her and saw the robe falling off one shoulder. Her skin was smooth, unblemished. He wanted to lick it, to slide that robe away.

No. He clenched his hands into fists. He had no right to touch her.

"I have to go. I don't belong here. Are you all right? Do you want me to call Indy?"

Arden clutched the robe edges together at her throat. "I'm fine. But... I want you to stay."

Those words sent emotions surging inside Dom. He wrestled with them and finally beat them down. His entire life, anything and everything he'd ever wanted had been denied to him. He was good at pushing his own needs away. Pushing his desires away.

Especially those things that he wanted to protect and take care of. "I can't stay."

Something flickered in her violet eyes. "You don't want to stay. I understand."

He reached out, his fingers touching her jaw in the lightest caress. He wanted to tell her that he wanted to stay more than anything he'd wanted in his entire life.

But he didn't. It was easier this way. He had no right to touch her.

He dropped his hand and her gaze lowered to the bed.

Dom rose, scooped up his armor off the floor, then strode to the door. He walked out without looking back.

Back in his quarters, he robotically showered and changed. He didn't let any thoughts penetrate. Not the smell of her, the sight of her bare shoulder, the feel of her pressed against him.

He'd just pulled on a shirt when the communicator beside his bed pinged. He touched the button. "Santora."

"Dom, it's Levi. The doc is just finishing up with the autopsy on the stealth raptor. Thought you might want to come take a look?"

"*Si*. Meet you there."

Grateful to focus on his job, Dom headed for the infirmary. As he reached the door, it opened, and a pregnant blonde strode out. The woman lifted her head, her mass of pale hair gleaming under the lights. Liberty was General Holmes' woman, and pregnant with their child.

Dom nodded at her.

She smiled at him. "Hello, there."

"Liberty. I hope you're well."

One manicured hand dropped to her belly. "Oh, the kiddo and I are doing very well. Of course, Adam is proving to be as overprotective as a daddy as he is as a general." She winked and continued down the hall.

When Dom stepped into the infirmary, he headed straight to the curtained-off examination rooms, and not the open area where the infirmary bunks were set up. In the first room, he saw the doc in her lab coat, bending over an autopsy table. She wore gloves up to her elbows, and they were streaked with blood. Like Liberty,

Emerson was also pregnant, and the mound of her belly was just starting to show.

All these babies. Dom didn't ever want to have kids. There was no way he would hand his DNA down to a child.

Marcus, Roth, Tane, Holmes, and Niko were all standing around the sides of the autopsy table, staring at the black raptor.

Emerson straightened, blowing a strand of straight, blonde hair out of her eyes.

"Stealth raptor is a good label for it," she said. "From what I can tell, it can distort its shape, which makes it easy for it to hide and sneak around."

"Fuck," Roth, the head of Squad Nine, muttered.

"Arden said it flowed," Dom said.

Everyone swiveled to look at him.

Emerson nodded. "Its skeletal structure is like gelatin. It seems it can harden and soften at will. So it can flatten itself, and then retake a solid form."

The general looked unhappy, staring at the raptor body with his arms crossed over his chest. "I want a way to detect this. I don't want these things slinking around the Enclave."

"Or getting inside," Niko said.

The doc nodded. "I'll send all my data through to Noah. I'm sure his team can come up with something."

"We need to end this," Marcus ground out. "Once and for all."

There were murmurs of agreement.

"We're working on that," Holmes said. "As soon as that bomb stops, we're going in to destroy it."

"I hear Noah's been working with Manu down in the armory," Tane said, mentioning his other brother. "They've perfected the cineole grenades and found a way to add the oil to weapons."

Cineole was a component of eucalyptus oil and the raptors hated it. They avoided Eucalyptus trees like they were the plague.

Holmes gave them a grim smile. "Our one bit of good news. And yes, we should have some experimental cineole weapons ready to use soon. Tane and Roth, keep your squads on alert for the bomb mission."

Roth and Tane nodded.

Then Roth turned to Dom. "Hey, thanks for rescuing Arden."

Dom lifted his chin. "No need to mention it."

"She's a hell of a comms officer, quiet, composed," Roth added. "And she's a good woman. Hate the idea the Gizzida could have nabbed her. She's been through enough."

She had. Walking away from her had been hard, but she deserved peace.

"Be nice if she found someone," Emerson said. "Heard on the base grapevine that she was seeing one of the schoolteachers."

The words were like a kick to Dom's gut. A teacher. He shoved his hands in his pockets. A steady man with no blood on his hands. That's exactly what Arden deserved.

For her, Dom would fight this attraction that tangled him up inside with all his strength.

CHAPTER FOUR

A rden's steps echoed on the concrete floor of the
empty firing range. As she and Noah entered,
Manu Rahia popped his head out of the office. He lifted a
hand at them.

"Hey, Noah, Arden." The tall man's voice was a deep
rumble.

He'd once been a berserker, fighting alongside his
brothers until he'd lost a leg on a mission. Now, he ran the
firing range and armory with skill and precision. Once
he'd adjusted to his prosthetic leg, he'd thrown himself
into his new role. And when he wasn't working, he was
with his lover, Captain Kate Scott, head of the Enclave's
security.

"Manu." Noah hefted up the combat drone in his
hand. "We're here to test out my work in progress."

"Place is all yours." Manu shifted, his black T-shirt
stretching over his broad, powerful chest. "Probably see a
few people come to shoot in about an hour."

"Thanks." Noah set the drone down, checking it over. Then his dark gaze hit Arden. "You sure you're up for this today?"

She sighed. "I'm fine. I wasn't hurt." She shook her head. "It was my own fault. I shouldn't have been outside."

Noah eyed her and nodded.

The drone beeped and rose up in the air.

"All right then, let's do this," he said.

Arden started walking around, passing the empty firing lanes. The drone followed.

"Target," she commanded.

The drone obeyed smoothly, lasers swiveling. She tested the functionality on several targets.

"I've programmed myself into the drone," Noah said. "Try targeting me."

"Are you sure that's a good idea?"

He shot her a pirate-like smile.

Arden smiled back. "Okay. Drone, target Noah Kim."

The drone lowered and turned, laser weapons locking on Noah.

He held up his hands like he was under arrest.

"Drone, disengage," she murmured.

The weapons retracted.

Noah strode over to a comp screen. "We'll try moving targets next and actually fire the lasers." His fingers swiped. "The simulation's all set."

Arden pulled in a breath. "Okay, drone, let's do this."

In the closest lane, holographic targets flashed up. The combat drone moved into action. It shifted fast, lasers firing.

She watched it take down each target and smiled. This could be a great new weapon to help keep the squads safer in the field.

"Holy hell," a deep voice said from behind her.

Arden swiveled and saw Griff and Dom. Her stomach danced and she met Dom's gaze.

"That's amazing." Griff was looking at the drone.

She ripped her gaze off Dom. "Drone, disengage."

"You're controlling it?" Dom frowned at her.

"Arden's implanted with a control chip," Noah said. "It's been slowly integrating with her nervous system, giving her greater control. We're still working out the kinks, but it's coming along very well."

Griff moved closer, lifting a hand to touch the drone. He started peppering Noah with questions.

"How are you?" Dom asked quietly.

Just looking at him made something inside her ache. He'd looked after her and she'd liked it, wanted more. But he'd just been being nice.

She tucked a loose strand of hair behind her ear. "Good. Fine. Thanks again for your help yesterday."

"Just doing my job."

Ouch. Arden fought to keep her face blank.

His gaze moved to the drone. "You're helping Noah with this."

"Noah needed a guinea pig and I was available. We've been working on it for a few weeks." She shrugged. "I wanted to help."

"You help every time you put on your headset and help keep your squad alive."

The praise made her cheeks heat. "You and the

35

others risk your lives out there every day. You're the heroes."

He shook his head. "Surely Noah could find a soldier to help with this drone."

"Soldiers are busy in the field or on patrol. I'm not." She paused. "It's safe."

"Well, there have been a few glitches," Noah said.

She glanced at the tech genius. "And you've worked them all out."

Noah raised a brow. "I still have to find a new desk to replace the one the drone fried in my lab yesterday."

Arden shot him a rueful smile. "Luckily, I ducked fast."

"You said it was safe." Dom's voice was cutting. "Noah, if that thing is blowing up desks, then Arden shouldn't be anywhere near it."

"It wasn't Noah's fault," she said. "Selena's bird came in and attacked the drone, causing the unexpected kerfuffle."

Dom frowned.

"The drone's safe. And just imagine once Noah's got a bunch of these perfected. They'll be so helpful for all the squads."

Noah nodded. "That's the plan. To have a combat drone attached to each squad."

"Nice." Griff glanced at Dom. "We'd better get shooting."

She watched the berserkers head over to their lanes. Griff was in jeans, but as usual, Dom wore black pants. She let herself have one quick glimpse at his perfect ass, then sighed.

She and Noah kept working on the drone, putting it through its paces. Finally, he nodded.

"Finished. Thanks, Arden."

"You're welcome." She watched him power it down.

He eyed her. "You should have dinner with Laura and me sometime."

"I'd like that."

With a wave, Noah hefted the drone and headed out. Not letting herself glance at the firing lanes, she headed out of the range.

"Arden."

Dom's voice made her quiver. She slowed and turned. She watched him stride toward her and something about him made her think of a stalking panther.

"I just wanted to make sure you're okay?"

She wrinkled her nose. "I wish everyone would stop asking that."

"No more sneaking out."

She held up a hand. "Believe me, I've learned that lesson."

Quiet fell between them and he kept staring at her. She stared back, drinking in his handsome face. Damn, it was hard having her long-dormant body flaring to life. Especially with a man who wasn't interested.

"Don't look at me like that," Dom ground out.

She blinked. Oh, God, he could read her like an open book. "Sorry, I..." She took a step back. "I know you aren't attracted to me, so you don't have to worry—"

He strode forward and she backed up until her shoulder blades hit the wall. Her hands went to his shoulders.

"Dom?"

"Don't want you?" His words were a deep growl.

She looked into his face and gasped. She saw heat in his eyes and her heart stopped. It wasn't a flicker of desire, but a deep, burning hunger. Pure need.

His hands slid into her hair and her lips parted.

Then he kissed her.

Oh. Her fingers clenched on him. Her world shifted.

She'd been kissed. She'd had good sex.

But right here, right now, Dom's kiss made her brain short-circuit.

His tongue thrust into her mouth and she kissed him back. The taste of him seared through her. The kiss wasn't slow or seductive, it was raw, deep, sexy. Her fingers twisted in his shirt.

Arden moaned.

The sound broke the spell.

Dom broke the kiss and stepped back. The space between them suddenly felt like a chasm. Arden pressed a palm to her racing heart, trying to catch her breath.

"I shouldn't have done that," he said.

She licked her lips. "Why?"

He shot her a dark, searing look.

She lifted her chin. "I liked it. I wanted it."

She saw his jaw tighten and one of his hands curled into a fist.

Suddenly, the firing range door opened and Griff strode out. "Dom. Squad's been called out."

Dom stiffened. "What's going on?"

"Tracker on the bomb stopped moving."

Arden gasped, just as her communicator beeped. She

pulled the small device out of her pocket. Then she looked up. "Squad Nine's been called out as well."

"APPROACHING LOCATION NOW."

Arden heard Indy's murmured words as they sat side by side in the Command Center. Squad Nine was currently flying their Darkswifts west of the tracker location, waiting to see if the berserkers needed them.

She prayed they didn't.

Indy wore her headset over her dark hair, her eyes glued to her comp screen. Arden, her throat tight, leaned over to see Indy's screen. It showed feed from Tane's helmet camera. He was walking, and she caught a glimpse of Hemi's broad shoulders.

As Tane moved again, she spotted Dom.

Arden's belly clenched. So dark and dangerous, carbine clutched with ease in his hands. His face was focused on the mission ahead.

He'd kissed her. She reached up and touched her lips. He'd set her body alight and made her ache.

Dom Santora was attracted to her. So why was he fighting it?

Indy's voice broke her out of her daydream. Arden cleared her throat. "Where are they exactly?"

Indy glanced up at her. "Just outside the town of Lithgow. About forty kilometers north-west of Katoomba."

Where they'd last seen the Gizzida bomb. The berserkers and Indy had barely survived with their lives.

The aliens hadn't moved very far.

"We're here," Tane said.

Arden gripped the edge of the table. She spotted the glimmer of water ahead.

"It's Lake Lyell." Indy tapped her screen. "Used to be a popular recreation spot for fishing, camping, water-skiing."

Arden could guess why the Gizzida had picked the location. While the northern edges of the lake were deeply forested, at the southern end, most of the trees had been cleared away. The raptors hated the Eucalyptus trees and the cineole chemical they emitted.

"What the fuck?"

Tane's curse made Arden glance back at the screen. She saw...something. Frowning, she leaned closer, staring at the large mounds lying at the lake's edge.

"What the hell?" Indy murmured.

Arden suddenly realized what she was looking at. She gasped. They were piles of decomposing bodies. Her stomach turned over. Heaps of bones, scales, skin.

"Shit, the stench," Levi muttered.

Tane turned his head, and Arden could see the piles continued into the distance along the water's edge, in both directions.

"Masks," Tane ordered.

Arden watched the berserkers pull small masks off their belts and slip them on. Then they moved closer to the piles of bodies. Some had spilled into the water and Arden pressed a hand to her mouth.

So many bodies.

Indy sucked in a breath, shaking her head.

Tane moved closer, aiming the camera downward. "The piles contain animals, humans, *and* raptors."

As Tane glanced around, Arden even made out the decomposing body of a rex. The carcass of the huge, tyrannosaurs rex-like alien was bloated and partially decomposed.

"It's a graveyard," Dom said. "Lots of human bodies have raptor scales."

"My guess is that they were test subjects who died in the Gizzida labs," Ash murmured.

Indy's face was pale, and Arden gripped the table harder. So many people had died in the Gizzida's horrible labs. To know they'd ended up here, tossed out like trash, was horrifying.

"Indy, how far away are we from the tracking signal on the bomb?" Tane asked.

"It's just a hundred meters west of your current location," Indy answered.

"I don't see anything," Tane said.

Arden kept watching, her body tense. The place was creepy. Wrong.

"Fuck," Hemi uttered.

"What is it?" Indy demanded.

"Some of the dead bodies are moving." Tane's voice was sharp. "Something's coming out of the piles."

Indy's screen flared to life with heat signatures. A lot of them. Arden gasped.

"Squad Three, you have—" Indy made a frustrated sound "—a fuckload of medium-sized heat signatures incoming."

"We see them."

Tane's voice was cool and controlled. On screen, dark shadows leaped out of the piles of bodies. They moved across the ground in a lightning-fast wiggle. They looked like giant worms.

They rushed at the berserkers.

Arden watched one of the creatures leap right at Tane. Indy and Arden had a clear view of the bottom of the alien—it had a wide, red sucker mouth. The thing looked like a giant leech.

Carbine fire erupted.

All around, more of the alien leeches were flinging themselves at the berserkers. The squad was cursing and fighting.

Arden touched her screen. "Roth, Squad Three are under attack by leech-like aliens."

"Acknowledged," Roth's deep voice responded. "We're headed their way."

"One touched my armor," Hemi yelled. "It's sizzling. Saliva is corrosive or poisonous, or something."

"Fuck." Indy was tapping furiously on the keyboard.

Arden watched more laser fire light up the sky. "They'll be okay, Indy. They're tough. And Nine's on the way."

Indy nodded, but her face was pinched.

Watching the fighting, Arden tried to keep her own worry hidden. *Come on, come on.* She knew that the berserkers were tough, excellent fighters. They fought hard and dirty. They'd be okay.

She searched the screen for any sign of Dom.

Then she heard Hemi's deep shout. "Fuck! Help."

"There's a sucker on Hemi," Levi yelled.

"Get it off me!" Hemi bellowed.

Tane was sprinting toward his brother and, on screen, Arden saw Dom leap over several bodies, knives in both hands.

Dom reached Hemi first. The bearded berserker was on the ground, wrestling with the giant leech attached to his chest. Dom dropped down, slashing at the sucker. As soon as he cut into it, it exploded. Gore flew everywhere.

Hemi sat up, roaring.

"Three more suckers incoming, Dom," Indy said frantically.

Arden pulled in a shuddering breath. She saw the horrible creatures slithering across the ground, honing in on Dom and Hemi. *Oh, God.*

CHAPTER FIVE

Dom gripped the neck of Hemi's armor and dragged the man aside. Hemi grunted, the side of his neck covered in nasty burns.

"Watch...out," Hemi bit out.

Turning, Dom saw another sucker rushing across the ground at them. He slashed out with his knife, the blade cutting into fleshy skin. It exploded.

Another creature leaped into the air, hungry mouth opening and closing. Dom thrust the knife in deep. *Splat.* He spun again and saw a third one slithering across the ground. He kicked it and when it flipped, he threw his knife at it.

Another explosion of gore. Dom scooped up his knife and shoved it back in its sheath. Then he gripped Hemi's armor and dragged the man away from the danger zone.

Ash raced over to help. The taller man grabbed Hemi from the opposite side, and together they set him down on the grass. Dropping to his knees, Ash yanked open his small med kit. He leaned over to treat Hemi's injury.

"Hang in there, my man," Ash murmured.

Dom straightened, scanning for more suckers. The front of his armor was splattered with gore, and steaming lightly.

The rest of the squad was firing. More suckers were racing across the ground from the piles of bodies. Dom tightened his grip on his knives. He'd always been good with the blade. He'd trained with knives ever since Salvatore had given him his first one as a boy.

Striding forward, he saw Tane and Levi spraying carbine fire. Griff kicked one of the suckers into the air. Then aimed his carbine and unloaded laser fire into it.

"There are more of them in the bodies," Griff yelled.

"Indy, we need back-up," Tane barked out.

"Squad Nine is on the way," Indy said in their earpieces.

Dom glanced over to check on Ash and Hemi. Ash had the other man on his feet, but Hemi looked like he'd been on a three-day bender, then lost a boxing match.

"Anyone see the bomb?" Dom searched the area.

"Dom, you're right near the signal." The voice in his earpiece didn't belong to Indy. It was Arden.

Her cool voice moved through him. He could easily picture her sitting in the Command Center. Hell, he could smell her, still taste her. He closed his eyes for a second. He was so weak.

When he opened his eyes, another sucker came at him. He bent low, his knife flashing. As the sucker's body disintegrated, he scanned the ground again.

"I can't see a bomb," Dom said.

"Motherfuckers." Suddenly, Hemi stepped forward and aimed his carbine. He sprayed laser fire around.

"Painkillers kicked in," Ash said dryly.

"Dom, behind you," Griff yelled.

Dom swiveled and spotted a sucker coming up behind him. He slammed his boot down on top of it. It twisted and made a hissing noise. He brought his knife down through its head.

It exploded.

Wincing, he yanked his knife out. He'd had enough blood and guts for the day.

Something glinted in the remnants of the sucker. *Cazzo.* He toed his boot through the mess.

"Indy, Arden. I found the tracker. It was in one of the suckers." It was corroded from being inside the alien. He crunched his boot down on it. They tried to never waste tech, but the tracker was damaged, and who knew if the Gizzida had hacked it. "The bomb's not here."

All around him, his squad mates cursed.

"Squad Three, mission fucking aborted," Tane said. "Let's get out of here."

"With pleasure." Levi stomped closer, his carbine still aimed at the corpses.

They all closed in, backing up together and moving away from the lake.

"I have the Hawk en route," Indy said. "Get back to the rendezvous point."

"I see the Darkswifts," Ash called out.

Dom glanced to the west and saw the dark shadows of the powered gliders in the sky above the far end of the lake. Then, as he took a step backward, his boot hit something wooden. He heard a splintering sound, and his foot dropped through.

Cazzo. His leg was stuck up to his knee. He jerked on it. It looked like someone had once dug some shallow tunnels that had been covered with wooden planks.

The wood cracked, and he fell down into the trench. Dom slammed onto his back, winded for a second. "Fuck!"

"Dom," Griff yelled.

His team mates appeared above him.

Dom sat up, then he froze. Something shifted in the darkness at the other end of the trench.

"Dom, get the fuck out of there." Griff's urgent voice.

Before he could get his feet under him, a mass of suckers rushed out of the darkness. His heart hammered in his chest. There were too many, and they were too close.

"Dom, get up." Arden's voice in his ear.

A sucker leaped on him. Dom slashed out with his knife.

But there were too many and they all landed on top of him in a writhing mass. Burning pain hit his face and neck. He heard his squad mates shouting.

"Get them off me!" Dom yelled.

One was right in front of his face. He grabbed it, tugging on its squishy body. Its flesh squeezed under his gloved fingers.

He sensed his squad close, fighting to free him, but he couldn't see a fucking thing. Another sucker latched onto his neck.

Dom shouted. Fiery pain tore through him, like being dipped in battery acid. Salvatore had liked to burn his enemies.

Blackness threatened, splotches dancing in front of Dom's eyes. His knife slipped from his hands.

"Dom, hold on!" Arden urged him.

Bella. It was a soundless whisper.

Then his familiar mistress, the darkness, sank her sharp claws into him and pulled him under.

———

WITH NAUSEA CHURNING in her gut, Arden clutched Indy's hand. They were running toward the Hawk hangar.

She knew her friend was worried about her entire squad. Arden sucked in a short breath, trying to ease the pressure in her chest. She was so worried about Dom.

As they reached the entrance to the hangar, Doc Emerson appeared. Behind her stood several of her nurses, pushing two iono-stretchers that floated above the ground.

Together, they stood in a small group.

"We'll get them all patched up." Emerson tried for a smile, tucking a strand of blonde hair behind her ear. "These berserkers are tougher than carbon fiber."

Arden couldn't smile back. She squeezed Indy's hand tighter. Dom was hurt badly. The others had pulled him out, but he'd been buried under a pile of suckers and unconscious.

And Tane had cut the camera feed, not letting them see him.

A moment later, the general joined them. He gave them a quiet nod, his face serious. "Squad Nine?"

Arden cleared her throat. "They provided cover for the berserkers to get back to the Hawk. They'll be landing shortly."

Alarms echoed through the cavernous hangar, followed by the clang of the doors above retracting. A second later, a Hawk quadcopter descended. The aircraft swiveled, and its skids touched the concrete floor.

Heart in her throat, Arden stared at the side door of the Hawk.

Be okay. Please, be okay.

The door slid open, and she instantly spotted Tane. He was always impassive and unsmiling, but now he looked downright grim.

Levi appeared, helping Hemi off. The man had nasty burns on his neck, and the chest plate of his armor was burned and twisted.

Then Ash and Griff followed, carrying a body between them.

Arden stopped breathing.

As she looked at Dom's limp form, flashbacks peppered her head. The night of the invasion. That night on the street, her family dead, so many injured, dead bodies all around her.

"Here." Emerson rushed forward, pushing an iono-stretcher. "Get him on here."

The men laid Dom out flat and a second later, Indy

threw herself into Griff's arms. Without thinking, Arden moved closer to the stretcher.

"I gave him a dose of nanomeds," Ash told the doctor.

Emerson clasped his shoulder. "Good work. We'll take it from here."

Arden pressed a fist to her chest, watching the doctor check Dom over and pressing medical monitoring patches to his skin. As Emerson shifted, Arden got a clear view of him.

Nausea rushed into her throat. His armor was completely ruined. What was left of it was peppered in burns, looking like it had melted. His face and neck were badly burned, all raw and red.

"I'm not lying on the damn stretcher," Hemi grumbled.

Emerson looked over and rolled her eyes. "Hemi Rahia!"

His face turned belligerent. "No."

Indy straightened. "I'll go and get Cam. She's on patrol."

Arden nodded, as her friend rushed off.

"All right, let's get Dom to the infirmary," the doctor ordered.

As the nurses started pushing the stretcher toward the door, Arden followed.

Once they reached the infirmary, Arden stayed to the side. They shifted him onto a bunk and she sat down beside his bed. The team worked around him—stripping his armor and cleaning his wounds. Arden reached out and touched his arm.

Emerson appeared. She eyed Arden, but didn't say

anything. She checked a scanner, making a few noises. She called out orders for some meds.

A moment later, the door opened and Hemi came in, sitting on a stretcher. A tall, dark-skinned brunette in armor was striding beside him.

"You're injured," Cam McNabb snapped. "You don't get to be an idiot. Whatever the doc tells you to do, you do it."

"Baby—"

"No way, Hemi Rahia. You're not *baby*ing me right now. I want you better."

As some of Emerson's team moved to work on Hemi, Emerson stayed close to Dom, checking his neck again. She glanced down at Arden.

Arden saw the silent question in the doctor's eyes. "I wanted to sit with him. He...helped me out recently."

Emerson nodded. "The nanos are working fine. His vitals are good. He's going to be okay."

The air shuddered out of Arden's lungs. "Thanks."

Finally, the medical team moved off, and there was quiet around Dom's bed.

Unable to stop herself, Arden reached out and stroked his face, where it wasn't injured. "The doc said you'll be fine."

She continued to murmur quietly to him, mostly nonsense stuff, but also letting him know he wasn't alone.

Suddenly, his dark eyes opened. They weren't very focused, but his head turned toward her.

"*Bella.*"

This close, she could see that his eyelashes were very long for a man and inky black. "I'm here."

His eyes closed and he was asleep again.

"How is he?"

Arden turned her head and saw Hemi—now fully healed—leaning heavily on Cam.

"He's resting. Doc Emerson said he's going to be fine. You?"

Hemi thrust a thumb against his chest. "I'm too tough to be down for long."

From beside him, Cam rolled her eyes.

"I'm going to head to my quarters and let my woman spoil me," Hemi said.

"Your woman's thinking of smacking you around for letting alien suckers hurt you," Cam amended.

Grinning, Hemi pulled her close, and Cam pressed her face to his chest and held him tight.

Then Hemi's gaze fell on Dom again and his smile faded.

"I'll stay with him," Arden said. "I owe him."

Hemi nodded. "Thanks, Arden."

"Take care."

Hemi and Cam headed out.

The hours ticked by, and Arden sat quietly in the chair, watching the ebb and flow of the infirmary. She kept an eye on Dom's monitors, ensuring everything was okay. Finally, he stirred.

He sat up, the sheet falling down his bare chest. The burns on his skin were almost healed.

"Thirsty." His voice was raspy.

Arden poured some water. "You're in the infirmary." Rising, she touched his bare shoulder and held the drink up to his lips.

He took a long sip, his gaze looking at her over the rim of the cup. "*Ciao*."

"Hi," she whispered back.

She set the drink down, and when she moved back to her chair, he reached out and grabbed her hand. His fingers circled her wrist, stroking her skin.

"Is everyone okay?" he asked.

"Yes."

"Hemi."

"All healed up, and no doubt letting Cam take care of him."

Dom shifted on the pillows. "You stayed with me."

They stared at each other.

"Yes," she said.

"Right-o." Emerson appeared. "Mr. Santora, you're my last task before I'm off to put my feet up and let my man massage them."

Arden tried to imagine big, silent, and scary Gabe from Hell Squad massaging the doctor's feet. Then she tried to work out how bubbly, friendly Emerson and Gabe worked.

But the pair were in love and—Arden's gaze dropped to the woman's belly—expecting twins, so clearly, they made it work.

"You're healing up nicely." Emerson peered at the monitors. "The nanomeds have just about finished up."

Arden sent up a silent thank you for the tiny medical machines that could heal just about any injury.

Emerson straightened, her hair swinging around her jaw. "You can go back to quarters, but I want someone with you to monitor you. These suckers have some new sort of poison in their saliva, and there's potential for there to be some lingering effects."

Dom frowned. "I'm—"

"I'll do it," Arden said. "I'll stay with him."

He scowled at her. "I don't need a—"

"Whatever he needs to do, I'll make sure he does it," she said firmly.

He grumbled something in Italian, dropping back against his pillows.

A smile curved Emerson's lips. "I'm sure you will. He just needs rest and some food. Keep him hydrated. Those suckers took a lot of blood."

"Then he'll rest," Arden assured the other woman.

Dom crossed his arms over his chest.

"I'll give you some painkillers," Emerson said. "You can give them to him if he has any additional pain."

"I *am* in the room," Dom said.

Arden ignored him and took the pills from the doctor. Whatever it took, she'd make sure he was okay.

DOM WOKE IN HIS BED. He glanced at the ceiling, carefully assessing his injuries. The pain in his neck had faded drastically, and it wasn't bad at all now. He'd lived with pain all his life, and learned to lock it down and not let it bother him.

He heard a faint scratching sound and turned his head on the pillow. Then he saw her, and the air caught in his chest.

Arden was curled up in the chair beside his bed, with

her feet tucked beneath her. Her sketchbook was resting in her lap, and she was busy sketching with a stick of charcoal.

He drank her in. His life had been void of good, clean beauty, and Arden encompassed all of that. Her hair was loose in shiny waves around her shoulders. Her elegant fingers were stained with black.

He shifted and she stilled, her gaze moving to his face.

"How are you feeling?" she asked.

"Like I got attacked by aliens and then healed up."

She watched him steadily.

"I'm fine." Dom sat up, the sheet pooling at his waist

He'd been injured before—by the Gizzida, by Salvatore's enemies, by Salvatore himself. He'd woken up plenty of times with various aches and pains. Not once could he remember anyone sitting by his bed.

Arden's gaze moved over his bare chest. Pink spots appeared in her cheeks.

"Keep sketching," he urged.

She was still for a second, then her hand started moving again. It didn't take long before she was absorbed in her work again. And then, after a few stolen glances, he realized that she was drawing him.

Dom leaned back, curling an arm behind his head. He heard her breathing hitch.

Hell, he was posing for her. He pulled in a breath and gave himself a mental shake. She wasn't for him. How many times did he have to keep reminding himself of that? His jaw tightened. He should push her away, drive her away, before he ruined her.

His hand clenched on the sheet, but he couldn't form any words.

He shifted again, and this time he felt a faint sting across his healing skin and winced.

"You're in pain. Emerson said that the residual poison from the suckers might prolong the pain." Arden rose, setting her sketchbook down on the bed.

"I'm used to pain."

She hesitated. "Your life before...it was dangerous."

Dom's hands clenched on the sheets. There were secrets he'd never told anyone. Secrets he kept locked away. But this woman was more dangerous than he'd guessed. She carved through his locks like a blade through skin.

"My earliest memory is being beaten. I stole some food." He heard her chest hitch. *Si*, he needed to make her see the gulf between them. "Growing up in a criminal organization means that pain is a way of life. Taking it—" he met her gaze "—and inflicting it."

She came unstuck and moved over to his kitchen. She grabbed a packet of medication off the counter. Then she filled a glass of water and returned. "No child should be beaten, in pain, or hungry."

Dom took the pills and their hands brushed. "I haven't been a child for a very long time."

She sat down on the edge of his bed.

A warning alarm blared in his head. Arden Carlisle anywhere near his bed gave his body ideas. Even now, barely healed, it was reacting to her. His blood pumped thickly through his veins.

He had to make her see. He had to protect her.

"Arden, why are you here?"

"I'm taking care of you."

"Why?"

She tucked some strands of her hair behind her ear. "Because I was worried about you."

"You shouldn't worry. You should stay far away from me."

Her nose wrinkled. "You aren't the big, bad, evil villain you pretend to be, Dom."

He sat up. "I'm not pretending anything. I was a Mafia enforcer, Arden." He lowered his voice. "You know what that means?"

She licked her lips. "Yes."

"You have no clue. What were you before the invasion?"

"An office manager."

"An office manager, with a regular job, a nice house, and a loving family."

She bit down on her bottom lip. "None of us are who we were before."

"I still kill. It's aliens now, but there was already blood on my hands."

She lifted her chin. "Stop trying to scare me."

"You should be scared." His hand flashed out and he grabbed her shirt, tugging her toward him. She gasped. He yanked her across the bed, their faces so close that their breath mingled. She was breathing fast.

Dom stroked the line of her jaw. "You can't handle me." His words were a growl.

He wanted to devour her whole. The things he wanted to do to her would terrify her.

"Dom." Desire vibrated in her voice.

He fought the urges in his body. He *wouldn't* destroy her. He pushed her away and watched as she caught herself before she fell off the bed. He had to fight himself to stop from reaching for her.

"Go, Arden. I might want to sink my cock deep inside you, but I don't want a needy, delicate woman who can barely cope with her own demons."

She looked like he'd struck her.

She stumbled backward off the bed. "Bastard."

Dom felt an ache in his chest, but he blocked it. *Pain.* There was always pain. That's all life ever brought him. "Yes, in the literal sense and the metaphorical one."

She stared at him, those big, violet eyes making him want to make mistakes.

Then she turned and ran out of his quarters.

Slowly, Dom shifted to the edge of the bed, dropping his head into his hands. She'd forgotten her sketchbook and it lay on his sheets. He reached out and opened it.

He saw the sketch of him lying on the bed and his gut clenched.

Then he flipped the page. The next picture was him in his armor. But she'd changed it. The armor was black, but it wasn't the sleek, modern carbon fiber they wore. She'd added details that made it look like the old-fashioned armor of a knight. And she'd put a sword in his hand.

Is that what she saw when she looked at him? No one would ever accuse him of being a knight.

The paper crumpled in his hand.

Then, the communicator beside his bed pinged.

Dragging in a deep breath, he leaned over and touched the button. "Santora."

"Dom?" It was Indy's voice. "How are you feeling?"

"Fine."

"Good. If you're up for it, there's a big meeting in the Command Center."

A distraction. Just what he needed. "I'll be there."

CHAPTER SIX

A rden stormed into her quarters. Her chest was viciously tight, and sadness was choking her.

Dom... *No*. She blocked him from her thoughts.

She moved into her bathroom and then stopped. She stared at her reflection in the mirror.

She looked so pale, so fragile. With one finger, she touched her cheek. She hadn't spent much time looking at herself in the mirror since the invasion. When had she become this delicate?

Sucking in a deep breath, she grabbed a hair tie and brush. Ruthlessly, she stroked the brush through her light-brown locks, then pulled her hair back in a ponytail. Then she splashed some water on her face.

When she looked up, there was a spark in her eye.

She had the right to grieve. She had a right to work through her loss. But dammit, even if she didn't like admitting it, there was a kernel of truth in Dom's words.

For the last two years, she'd been existing. She'd

stopped living the day she'd lost her family. And some-where along the line, for better or worse, she'd let herself forget that she was still alive.

Arden lifted her chin. Still, he was an asshole to talk to her like he had.

Her communicator dinged and she strode back into the main room. She saw a message and thumbed the button. She quickly read the text. There was a meeting in the Command Center.

Lifting her chin, she strode back into her bathroom and tore open the drawers. She found the small case Indy had given her and yanked out some lip gloss. It was a pretty, bright pink. She swiped some on, then headed out of her quarters.

As she headed down the corridor, she felt...pissed. Anger was swelling inside her. Anger at a dark, hand-some asshole.

When she reached the Command Center, she found it packed. All the squads were inside—muscled bodies and broad shoulders taking up space—along with the Command Center staff.

She spotted Roth's dark head, and moved toward Squad Nine. As she neared, Taylor looked up and smiled. The woman's gaze moved over Arden's body.

"You look...different," Taylor said.

Arden shrugged in response. "What's going on?" There was an edgy vibe in the room.

Taylor shook her head. "The general's about to share."

Up front, Holmes clapped his hands. "Everyone, listen up." The composed man blew out a breath. "Several minutes ago, the drone team picked up an explosion in the Blue Mountains."

Gasps and murmurs ran through the crowd.

"It occurred north of Katoomba."

Arden's body locked. *Oh, God. The bomb.*

"We're currently waiting for intel, and have a drone en route."

Everyone turned to the giant screen on the wall. It flickered, and footage from a moving drone appeared. The machine was racing over a sea of green trees.

Arden glanced around the room. Everyone's attention was glued to the screen. Then, she spied Dom standing with the berserkers and her heart bumped hard against her ribs.

As she looked at him, he turned away from the screen and his gaze locked with hers.

She quickly glanced away.

"Coming in now," Lia said.

The woman was seated behind a comp screen up front. The head of the drone team was currently in command of the drone. The woman had a deft touch with the machines.

"It's in the community of Mount Wilson," Lia added.

Arden started. "I remember Mount Wilson. There's a small survivor community there."

Lia frowned, glancing Arden's way before turning back to her screen. Her long fingers manipulated the controls in a calm, competent fashion.

"You're correct, Arden." Lia flicked a glance at Holmes. "They didn't want to leave and come to either

Blue Mountain Base, or the Enclave when we moved it. It's been a while since we last checked in with them."

The small town came into view.

And so did the carnage.

Plumes of smoke rose above the trees. Trees were burning, houses were destroyed, the ground was churned up.

Arden pressed a fist to the center of her chest. Around her, the room echoed with curses.

"Fuck me."

"Hell."

"Shit."

The drone swept in closer.

People were staggering around the street, and her pulse jumped. They were still alive. But as the footage zoomed in closer, a bad taste coated her tongue. Most were limping, some were crawling along the ground. Screams and moans filled the speakers.

The general stiffened. "Squad Nine, Squad Three, I'm going to send you in. Get prepped—"

"Wait." Lia's horrified voice. "Look."

Arden saw it, too.

The people had patches of scales on them. It looked like someone had splattered them with raptor scales.

As they watched, a man fell to the ground, writhing. He had scales covering his left arm, and, as they watched, his body twisted, the scales seeming to flow over his chest. His body was transforming, right before their eyes.

"It was the test bomb," Noah murmured from the front. "There it is. The raptors set off the test bomb."

She followed to where Noah was pointing, and saw

the remnants of the small bomb now. It was made of black metal, about the size of a dining table. It was shaped like an octagon, with lots of sharp angles. It looked like the top of it had burst open, and parts of it were melted.

"Tane, Roth, go," the general ordered. "We need samples and images. We need to know what the hell happened."

Emerson pushed forward. "General, people are hurt—"

Looking like a heavy weight was sitting on him, Holmes shook his head. "We can't send a medical team into that. Equip the squad medics with what you think they might need."

A rumble of conversation swelled in the Command Center, full of anger, shock, and disbelief. The berserkers strode out the doors, their faces set. Arden stared at the back of Dom's white shirt.

Then she swiveled and saw Roth nod at his squad.

"Roth, I can help." Arden gripped the man's arm. "I've been working with Noah, testing the new combat drone he's developed. It's linked to me. It has weapons and full recording capabilities—"

Roth scowled. "It's too dangerous."

"The drone is incredible," she insisted. "It has scanning abilities. We can gather data from the entire town. Roth, those people are *turning* into Gizzida. We need to know exactly what happened. I want to help."

From beside Roth, his second-in-command, Mac, nodded. "Arden makes a good point. The combat drone could help."

The squad leader shoved a hand through his hair. "I'll control it—"

Arden shook her head. "I have a control chip implanted, and I've been training with it. It's taken weeks to get to the point I'm at. There isn't time."

"We'll keep her safe," Mac said.

Roth blew out a breath, but nodded. "Okay, let's move."

Eagerness racing through her, Arden headed over to Noah. "I'm going with my squad. We need the combat drone."

The man's eyes narrowed. "You sure?"

She nodded. "Absolutely. I can help."

Noah grabbed her arm. "It's going to be bad out there, Arden. You'll be up close and personal with it."

She dragged in a breath. "I know. I can handle it."

He eyed her for a second, then gave one decisive nod. "I'll get the drone. I'll also program all the squad members into it. Meet you at your locker room."

"Thanks, Noah."

Arden went with her squad. Taylor and Sienna helped deck her out in armor.

"You're closer to my size," Sienna said, holding up an armor plate. "But taller." The woman strapped it onto Arden.

"Here." Taylor handed over a small thermo pistol. "Hope you won't need it, but pays to be prepared."

The armor felt too big and bulky, like she was a kid playing dress-up. She slid the pistol into the holster at her hip. Around her, the rest of the squad were almost finished getting their gear on. Theron and Roth were talking quietly, Mac and Cam were checking their weapons, and Taylor and Sienna were pulling on the last of their armor.

Arden pulled in a steadying breath. Her squad never hesitated to go out there. To help and risk their lives for others. People were dying, and they needed to know everything they could about this bomb.

Or every single person in the Enclave could be next.

Noah met them in the corridor. He held the large drone in one hand. "You sure you want to do this?"

Arden nodded. "I'm sure."

He activated the drone and it rose up in the air. It moved to Arden, hovering above her, lights blinking.

"That is so awesome," Mac murmured.

"Good luck." Noah gripped Arden's shoulder. "See you when you get back."

She walked to the Hawk hangar with Squad Nine, the drone moving behind her. She saw the berserkers were already prepped and standing beside their Hawk, checking their weapons.

When Dom lifted his head and saw her, his brows drew together.

"What is she doing here?" He stabbed a finger at Arden.

She stepped forward, and the drone above her shoulder, followed her. "*She* is going on this mission."

Dom swiveled to Roth. "And you're on board with this?"

"Not entirely," Roth said. "But Arden is linked to the new combat drone, and—"

"This is a fucked up idea," Dom snapped.

"Dom," Tane said in a warning tone.

"This has nothing to do with you, Dominic Santora." Arden swiveled and stomped toward her squad's Hawk. Without looking back at him, she climbed aboard.

DOM WAS BEYOND PISSED.

Rage coiled in his belly, and the worst Italian curses he could think of filled his head. He gripped a handhold above his head as the Hawk took off.

Bubbly pilot Maddy was in the cockpit today. The woman was young but she could fly.

As soon as they were up in the sky, Dom glanced out the side window and saw the other Hawk beside them. Arden was on there. *Cazzo.*

"Not like you to lose your cool like that, Santora," Tane noted.

Dom stayed silent. Arden was heading into the field, into enemy territory.

"You got something going on with the pretty comms officer from Nine?" Hemi asked.

Dom turned his head and found his squad all watching him. Griff's gaze was on him like a laser beam.

"No," Dom answered. "I just don't think it's a good idea to send an untrained civilian into this cluster fuck. We don't even know what we're facing down there."

Tane didn't reply, but the others nodded. Most of them had been forced to take their women into the field at some stage. Indy and Selena had both played a part during the fucked-up mission in Katoomba.

"Well, did you see that combat drone?" Hemi said. "It looked badass."

"That's not the goddamned point, Hemi," Dom said with a growl.

"Dom," Tane said.

Dom held up a hand. "I'm fine. I just haven't forgotten carrying a blood-splattered Arden inside after we saved her from that stealth raptor." Or the way he'd hurt her. Used words to dig at her old wounds.

Levi grunted. "She was freaked."

Dom dragged in a breath. "I'm focused on the mission."

And he'd keep one eye on Arden's slim ass while he was doing it.

"Approaching Mount Wilson," Maddy called back. "Ready to do your thing, bad boys?"

"We're ready, baby," Hemi called back.

They landed in a clearing, just outside the town.

As Dom's boots hit the dirt, he saw Squad Nine was already out of their quadcopter, and moving into formation. Arden stood beside Taylor, the combat drone hovering in the air nearby.

Roth pointed and Tane nodded. Both squads moved forward.

Arden stared straight ahead, not looking at Dom.

Dom focused on putting one boot in front of the other. He'd done the right thing, pushing her away. He hated that he'd used her grief to do it, but the woman was quickly burrowing under his skin. He had to save her from getting in too deep with him.

As soon as they moved into the main street of the

town, the smell of smoke and burning filled his nostrils. Moans reached his ears.

"Stay sharp," Roth murmured.

They all had their carbines up, their bodies tense.

Arden's drone swiveled, scanning the street.

"Help...us."

Dom turned. Two people were dragging themselves along the ground, toward the squads.

One, a woman, reached out a hand. Pain was etched on her face, but her eyes glowed a deep, hungry red.

"Hold," Roth said.

Dom stopped, as did everyone else. But he could see that it was costing them all. Each one of them wanted to run over and help.

Suddenly, the people on the ground hissed, their faces twisting. The door of a nearby house slammed open, and two more hybrid humans rushed out.

They came in fast, their faces half skin, half scales, and they both had glowing, red eyes. As the pair raised their hands, he saw their fingers were now claws.

The pair let out guttural roars and attacked.

One was close to Arden. She staggered back, throwing her hands up.

Dom swiveled and fired.

Carbine fire erupted, both squads opening fire. The two contaminated hybrids collapsed.

"Fuck." Tane moved closer to look. "Don't get too close to the others."

The two on the ground started snarling, their eyes flashing.

"Can we save them?" Arden asked, horror in her voice.

Dom swallowed against the lump in his throat. They'd seen this before, people infected with Gizzida DNA. But those humans had been trapped in the aliens' labs and were being experimented on.

He knew once a human was infected, and the Gizzida DNA took hold, there was no way back. Doc Emerson and her team had been trying, but hadn't found a way to reverse the transformation.

Ash shook his head, a muscle in his jaw ticking. "There's nothing we can do for them."

Arden's drone darted forward. Laser fire shot out, and the two people on the ground stopped moving.

Dom glanced at her. She stood nearby, her face pale and set.

"Come on." Tane stepped forward.

The two squads moved quietly down the street, encountering more twisted, mutated dead bodies.

A lot of them.

Two more Gizzida hybrids attacked, and Levi and Ash turned to deal with them.

The teams approached the remnants of the test bomb.

"We need pictures," Roth ordered.

"My drone is recording," Arden said.

Mac pulled out a small camera. "I'll take a few extra, as well."

Tane touched his ear. "Indy, I can confirm that the test bomb was detonated. It looks like it's spread Gizzida

DNA everywhere. Everyone in the town is already well into the change to a hybrid."

"Fuck." Indy's tone was shaky.

Dom stared at the black metal remnants of the bomb. This one was small, but he knew that somewhere out there, the raptors had a much larger version. One designed to do exactly this, but on an immense scale.

It made him feel sick.

This was the aliens' final weapon. One to rid the Earth of the last of the pesky human survivors. One that would turn every single one of them into Gizzida.

Dom ground his teeth together. Fuck that.

Arden's drone moved fluidly through the air, scanning and taking pictures. He saw her step away from the group, moving toward a house that looked mostly intact.

Out on the front lawn, he watched her drop to her knees.

Driven by a need he couldn't fight, he moved toward her. As he got closer, his gut twisted.

Two smaller bodies lay on the overgrown grass. Both were fully covered in thick, gray scales, their faces twisted and deformed.

Kids. They'd just been kids. Probably pre-teens.

Arden knelt there, staring at them. Unmoving.

Dom reached out and touched her shoulder.

She didn't look up at him, but she lifted a hand and grabbed his. He tightened his fingers on hers.

Pain and rage vibrated off her.

Suddenly, the front door of the house burst open, and a woman staggered out. She saw the bodies and dropped to her knees.

"My babies," she wailed.

Arden trembled, then pushed to her feet. She approached the woman.

"Arden," he warned.

She ignored him. "I'm sorry."

The woman lifted her face. She looked like she was a few years older than Arden. Life had lined her face, and her dark hair, threaded with gray, was tangled.

"My babies." A harsh, broken exclamation.

The woman had a tiny patch of scales on her cheek, but otherwise appeared untouched.

"My partner hid us when the aliens came." The woman looked around wildly. "I fell in the basement and hit my head. When I woke up, Annie and Mickey were gone."

"I'm sorry," Arden whispered.

The woman's face collapsed. "They're gone." As she broke into sobs, Arden wrapped her arms around the woman, and shared her grief.

"They aren't hurting anymore," Arden whispered.

Dom looked at Tane. "Survivor. Only a small touch of scales."

Tane nodded. "We'll take her in."

Dom nodded, his gaze moving back to Arden's pale-brown hair. She held the woman, tears tracking down her cheeks. He didn't look at the smaller bodies again, but Dom vowed that he would make the Gizzida pay.

CHAPTER SEVEN

Arden felt icy cold as she sat on the Hawk. She was wedged in between Taylor and Sienna, but she couldn't feel any warmth.

Around her, the squad was talking, but the mood was somber.

The survivor, Alyssa, sat silently at the back of the Hawk with Mac, a blanket wrapped around her hunched shoulders. Arden understood the grief she saw etched on the woman's face. Every single bit of it.

Arden looked away. She'd powered down the drone, and it sat on an empty seat behind her. She couldn't believe the devastation she'd seen at Mount Wilson. That any species could be so callous. Those poor people, twisted and deformed.

Those small bodies...

She squeezed her eyes closed. She sat there in silence, the icy grip tightening, deepening.

It was only when she felt the Hawk start to lower that

she realized they were back at the Enclave. Staring wood-enly out the window, she saw the rock walls blur past.

"We're home." Sienna rubbed Arden's back, her gaze flicking up to her man, Theron, who was standing nearby.

As soon as Roth pushed the door open, Arden spotted Indy standing outside the Hawk. Her friend looked worried.

Arden reached the door and climbed off the Hawk.

"Hey," Indy said.

Arden nodded.

Noah appeared. "Good work out there with the drone."

Arden cleared her throat. "The drone's in the Hawk—"

He nodded. "I'll get it and start downloading the data you collected."

She nodded again, watching as he climbed into the Hawk. When he reappeared, he was holding the drone in one hand.

The alarms sounded again, and she knew the berserkers' Hawk was incoming.

Indy wrapped an arm around Arden's shoulders. "Come on."

"Alyssa—"

"Will be taken care of," Indy said.

Without saying another word, Arden let her friend whisk her away. She wasn't even sure what route they took, but soon Indy was leading Arden into her quarters.

Indy nudged her toward the bathroom. "Go and have a hot shower. Your skin feels like ice."

Like an automaton, Arden stepped into the bathroom and closed the door. She stripped her armor off, then her clothes. She turned on the shower and stepped under the hot spray, lifting her face up to the water.

Then the tears fell.

She didn't make a sound, just let the tears flow quietly down her face. She stayed there until she felt the water start to cool.

She finally shut off the shower, dried herself, and wrapped the towel around her body. She saw Indy had snuck in and left some clean clothes resting on the edge of the bath tub. A long, flowing skirt in a deep navy blue, and a simple white top.

Too tired and heartsick to care what she wore, Arden slipped the clothes on. When she entered her main quarters, Indy was making toast and tea in the kitchenette.

"Here." Indy set a plate and mug down on the table.

Arden sat in a chair and stared at the food. She wasn't hungry.

"You okay?" Indy asked.

Arden tried to fight off the despair eating at her insides. She grabbed her friend's hand. "There were dead children, Indy."

"I know." A soft whisper.

"That woman, Alyssa...she's me."

"She's not you, but you understand what she's going through."

"I'm not all right." Arden blew out a breath. "But I will be, eventually."

Indy squeezed her hand. "You are one of the strongest people I know."

Arden gave a choked laugh. "Me?"

"You. You survived the worst of circumstances, but now, you've found your way to honor those you loved. To remember them, and remember that you're still alive."

"Thanks, Indy."

"Of course." Her friend's gorgeous eyes flashed. "Friends take care of friends."

"Not just for that." Arden tucked a strand of damp hair back. "For being my friend. For pushing closer when I tried to hold you back."

Indy tilted her head. "You're quieter in general, and you were grieving, I knew that. I liked you anyway."

And Indy was bold, a force of nature. She'd kept pushing until Arden had no choice but to let go of the gray and embrace Indy's color.

"I love you," Arden said.

Indy hugged her. "Right back at you, babe."

Arden sat up straighter. "Now, go be with your guy." Griff would be champing at the bit to get his hands on his woman.

Indy hesitated.

With another squeeze, Arden released Indy's fingers and curled her hands around her tea. She wasn't hungry or thirsty—in fact, she was pretty sure her stomach would rebel—but she forced herself to take a sip. *Gah*. As always, Indy had piled the sugar in. But Arden wanted to reassure Indy that she was doing okay.

"Go."

Her friend let out a breath. "Fine. By the way, I found your sketchbook slipped under the door." She pointed to the table. "I put it over there for you."

Arden felt a flash of something in her chest. The sketchbook she'd left in Dom's quarters. "Thanks."

After another hug, Indy left. In silence, Arden finished the tea and managed a couple bites of the toast. Her gaze moved back to her sketchbook. He'd returned it. Probably known she'd feel the need to draw, to release the horrors she'd seen. Damn him for seeing her so clearly.

She wanted to be okay. She wanted to be like her squad mates and shake off what she'd seen. God, the squad soldiers went out there every day and saw horrible things. Terrible, nightmarish things. And they had to fight and kill.

Her stomach turned over. She felt like the walls were closing in on her.

She needed air.

She needed to get out of there.

Arden jumped to her feet, then snatched up her sketchbook and pencil case, and a soft black blanket off the back of her armchair. She slipped on some shoes and rushed out of her quarters. She started off down one corridor, then realized abruptly she was heading to one of the concealed exits to outdoors. No. She made a one-hundred-and-eighty-degree turn. She'd made that mistake once and she wouldn't do it again.

Not only had she risked her own life, she'd risked Dom and Levi's. Forced Dom—a man who'd already killed too much—to take a life again.

She charged through corridors, avoiding anyone who wanted to talk. Eventually, she found herself in the corridor leading to the Garden. After a short ride on the automatic train, she stepped through the doorway into the big, open bowl that had been cut into the top of the escarpment above the Enclave.

As she breathed in the lush scent of flowers and green grass, her racing pulse calmed. It was dark, but the retractable roof was open, and above her, stars twinkled in the vast expanse of space. She caught a glimpse of the round orb of the rising moon.

Looking up, she pulled in some deep, calming breaths. She kicked her shoes off and walked onto the grass, feeling her toes sink into it. Right here, right now, it was easy to imagine that the invasion had never happened. That adults and children had never died.

That her family hadn't been lost.

Arden wandered deeper into the trees. On one side of the Garden were the neat rows of thriving vegetable plants that helped feed the Enclave. The other side was for recreation, and a safe place for the residents to get some sunshine during the day. Trees were scattered through the thick grass, and there was a large children's play area, and several picnic tables.

A strange noise caught her ear and she frowned. *Thwap. Thwap.* Darn, she'd wanted the place to herself.

She circled a tree and her steps faltered.

Dom. He'd showered and was wearing dark pants, and a white, button-down shirt that glowed like a beacon in the darkness. The other berserkers usually dressed like bikers—jeans and T-shirts. But Dom always wore pants and crisp shirts. She liked it. A lot.

She watched him lift an arm and throw something.

The moonlight glinted off the knife as it flew through the air, embedding itself firmly in the trunk of a tree.

He lifted his arm and took aim again.

Arden drank him in. The fluid way his body moved as he tossed the knife. His skills were evident.

She didn't think she'd made a sound, but suddenly, his head whipped around. His gaze moved to her face.

"Couldn't sleep?" he asked.

She shook her head.

"Me, neither."

She tilted her head. "But you told me you'd seen this all before. You told me that it's all you know. Death, dying, killing..."

He strode over to the tree that was his target, and this time, his movements were jerky. He yanked the knives out.

He still felt it. Her lips firmed. He wasn't indifferent to the suffering. Everything he saw still hurt him.

Dom Santora was a fraud.

He was just as haunted by his demons as she was, and he used them like a shield to keep people at bay.

He turned back to her and his gaze dropped to her sketchbook. "Are you going to draw?"

She nodded. She didn't let herself think, and suddenly the words were tumbling out of her mouth. "Will you pose for me?"

He stilled. She was sure he was going to say no.

"You owe me," she said. "For being an asshole this morning."

"People have called me far worse." He looked at the

grass, his voice lowering to a whisper. "I am sorry I hurt you."

Arden suspected that Dom hadn't apologized to many people before. She laid out her blanket. "You can lie on that."

Then she pulled back a few meters and dropped down onto the grass, tucking her skirt beneath her. She flicked open her sketchbook.

Dom set his knives down, then knelt on the blanket.

"Take your shirt off," she ordered.

He glanced over at her. In the shadows, the stark lines of his face were even more severe. He looked darker and more dangerous than usual.

His hands lifted and he unbuttoned his shirt. *Yes.* Arden fought back a little smile. With each inch of bronze skin he uncovered, desire unfurled in her.

The shocking warmth of the sensation started to melt away the ice the mission had left inside her.

Dom dropped his shirt on the grass, then he lay back on the blanket. He propped himself up on one elbow.

He was gorgeous. A dark knight at rest. All that lean muscle was delectable, and she studied the dark ink on his hip. She wanted to ask him what it was, but she was too afraid to ruin the moment.

Arden snatched up her charcoal and started drawing. The desperate urge to capture the moment, to capture him, welled up. As her hand moved, her tense muscles started to relax. Even as her hand moved faster, she felt calmer, smoother.

"Lean back more," she ordered. "You've just returned from battle and you're taking a well-deserved break."

He eyed her for a beat, then leaned back. The hard muscles in his abdomen flexed.

She blew out a breath. It still wasn't quite right. Could she—?

Arden lifted her head, and took a chance. "Can you take the rest of your clothes off?"

Her words fell into silence. He just stared at her, his face unreadable.

She swallowed against her dry throat and stared back at him.

Then he pushed himself up and rose. With slow, methodical movements, he unfastened his trousers. Her breath hitched. In one quick move, he shucked his pants and black boxers off.

Her chest went solid. He sank back down and reclined on the blanket again.

Oh. God.

Every inch of him was perfection. As he lay there, she sketched his sleek flank and the one hard cheek of his ass that she could see. His legs were powerful and muscled.

She let herself look at the faint shadow of his cock.

She bent her head over her paper, sketching fast. He was pure, masculine beauty and she had to capture it all.

"Turn a little more toward me," she said.

He shifted. And now she had a perfect view of his cock. She swallowed. He was hard, his cock, thick and full.

Arden felt a rush of wet between her legs. She clenched her thighs, her pulse throbbing under her skin.

She kept sketching.

The dark knight had survived the fight. Now, he was home, his body raging with need.

As she studied the image on her paper, filling in some detail with her charcoal, she sensed him move.

She lifted her head and the air rushed out of her.

He'd curled one strong hand around his cock, giving it one hard pump. Her belly clenched and she sucked in a harsh breath.

"Watch, Arden." His voice was a harsh growl as he stroked his cock. "Watch what you do to me."

CAZZO. Dom stroked himself. His cock was as hard as steel. He could feel Arden watching him, and desire was coiling at the base of his spine, waiting to strike.

He looked at her face. Her lips were parted, her gaze on his cock. Her body was shifting restlessly on the grass.

"You are so beautiful," she breathed.

He blinked. No one had ever called him beautiful before. "Not as beautiful as you."

Her eyelashes fluttered. "I've heard pretty and attractive, but no one's ever called me beautiful, either."

It was more than just her looks. It was the inner sense of calm and caring that emanated from inside her. Dom had learned at a very young age to know when a pretty face hid kindness, or rot. If someone would help you, or hurt you.

He stroked again, a groan tearing out of him. He heard her breathing hitch.

"How do you feel?" he asked.

"Hot," she confessed, shifting again.

"Pull up you skirt, Arden."

She shivered, then tentatively, reached down. Her fingers slid over her skirt and wadded the fabric. Dom's pulse jumped. She started pulling the material up slowly, baring slender legs inch by inch.

Her skin gleamed in the moonlight. She pulled the fabric up to her thighs.

"*Bella*. See what you do to me." He canted his hips forward.

Her gaze was glued to his hard cock.

"Touch yourself," he murmured.

She swallowed. With the hand not stained with charcoal, she reached under the hem of her skirt. She made a small sound that made heat break out over his skin.

"Slide your pantics aside. Stroke yourself."

She obeyed, her head falling back like it was too heavy for her neck.

"That's it. You're gorgeous." His cock throbbed intensely. It wouldn't be long before he was spilling all over himself.

Her legs shifted, and he watched her hand move faster.

"How do you feel?" he asked. "Are you wet?"

She nodded. "Yes. So wet."

Her eyes locked with his. She kept stroking. Both of them stroking together.

"That's it, Arden."

"Oh. Oh—" Her eyes widened.

"Let go, *bella*."

Suddenly, she cried out, the noise echoing through

the trees. It took all of Dom's control not to rush over to her. To push her down on the grass, to taste her, touch her, and cover her body with his.

Her head fell forward and she was panting.

"Beautiful," he said.

She lifted her head, looking at him. He was stroking his cock faster now.

Then she moved, launching herself forward and crawling across the grass to him.

He stiffened. "Arden—"

Slender hands touched his, surrounding his cock. At the brush of her skin, he groaned, his hips pushing upward.

"You're beautiful, too." Her voice was husky.

They stroked his cock together, and he felt his orgasm bearing down like a hunter with the scent.

And then before he knew what she had planned, she ducked her head toward his lap. He sucked in a sharp breath, and then she wrapped her mouth around the swollen head of his cock.

Dom's groan was ripped violently out of him. The hot feel of her mouth combined with the suction almost made him come, then and there. He looked down, and seeing her hair spilling over his thighs almost finished him off.

She licked him and then sucked him deep.

"Arden... Wait..." He sank a hand in her hair, but kept his grip gentle. He never wanted to hurt her or scare her.

She sucked harder, pulling him deeper into her mouth.

DOM

Sensations exploded inside him.

With a roar, Dom came. Arden swallowed him down, her fingers digging into his hips. Lights blinked behind his eyes, and pleasure tore him apart and put him back together.

When he could think again, his lungs were working like bellows. He tried to scrounge up some control. Arden pulled back, licking her lips. Her face was flushed.

He growled. All thoughts flew out of his head and he reached for her. She let out a small cry, hands clinging to his shoulders.

He pushed her back on to the blanket, his hands twisting in her skirt.

"Dom—"

"Quiet."

His growl had her stilling. He wrenched her skirt up to her waist and she gasped.

"My turn," he said.

She shook her head. "I won't come again—"

"You will."

He lowered his head and kissed her thigh. She jumped.

Then he shoved the soaked gusset of her panties aside. His tongue was on her, and she moaned.

Her hands clamped into his hair hard enough to hurt, but he didn't care. He stabbed his tongue inside her, savoring the taste of her.

"Dom!"

He worshiped her. He had Arden under his mouth, her taste in his senses. Arden. Sweet Arden. She writhed beneath his lips.

He used his tongue, lips, and teeth to pleasure her. Every cry, he felt deep in his body. He circled her clit and she moaned. She tasted like heaven. He kept licking and sucking.

"Dom. *Dom*." Her voice broke.

Then she arched and cried out his name. Her body shook wildly as she came again.

His. Dom had never in his life owned anything. Never had anything that was solely his. Never had anything worth keeping.

But his name on Arden's lips, her body shaking from the pleasure he could give her—he wanted that. Forever.

He pulled her into his arms, curled his body around hers, and held her tight.

CHAPTER EIGHT

The sunshine woke Arden. She blinked and realized her nose was pressed to a hard chest covered in warm skin.

Her eyes popped open.

God, she was wrapped around Dom. They were still lying on the blanket, and his trousers were back on, but he was shirtless. There was so much glorious bronze skin on display.

Memories of what they'd done the night before filtered through her head and she trembled.

Dark eyes opened.

"Good morning." His voice was a deep rumble.

"Morning." She instantly felt heat in her cheeks.

He lifted a hand and touched her hair. Then he moved his head, pressing his lips to hers. The kiss was slow, soft.

Just as she was reaching for him, a loudspeaker blared.

"Attention Enclave residents." General Holmes' voice came through the speaker.

Dom cursed, his arms tightening on her. Then he sat up, pulling her with him.

"This is General Holmes. All adults are to attend a meeting in the dining room now. I repeat, all adults to the dining room now. Thank you."

Arden's hands clenched on Dom's skin. This couldn't be good.

"Come on." He rose, pulling her up to stand beside him.

Arden straightened her skirt and tried to smooth the wrinkles in her shirt. They were both rumpled. Dom turned and for the first time, she got a clear view of his back. Her belly clenched. There were a few old scars, but what drew her gaze was his tattoo. On his upper back, along his spine, was a beautiful dagger done in stark black ink.

She wanted to touch it. Her hands twisted in her skirt. She wanted to sketch it.

Then he pulled on his shirt and buttoned it, the tattoo out of view.

"Here." He reached up and plucked something from her hair. "You had some grass there."

"Thanks."

She scooped up the blanket and her sketchbook. When she straightened, Dom cupped her cheek, his thumb sliding across her cheekbone.

Her insides melted. "Dom—"

"We'll talk later, *bella*."

She nodded. He took her hand, leading her to her shoes, then he tugged her out the door.

"What do you think the general's going to say?" she asked.

Dom frowned. "I guess that they've had a chance to analyze the data from your drone. They must have more information on the bomb."

A cold shiver skittered down her spine. They made a quick detour so Arden could drop off her things. By the time they made it to the dining room, the large space was packed.

Even Gaz'da was present. Their resident Gizzida—one who'd defected and managed to turn away from his Gizzida programming—was a useful ally. He'd helped them out numerous times, and usually stayed to himself. He spent most of his time with Laura and her team in the interrogation area.

Still, looking at the alien made Arden uneasy. She knew he was a victim as well, but her memories of the invasion and all the times her squad had fought the raptors were too twisted up in her head.

General Holmes was standing at the front of the room. He grabbed a chair and stepped up onto a table.

"Okay, quiet, please." Holmes scanned the room. "Yesterday, the raptors detonated a test bomb." He took a deep breath. "We collected samples and data, and questioned the lone survivor."

Tension filled the room and Arden heard fearful whispers.

"Our witness overheard some of what the Gizzida had to say before she hid. The bomb was filled with

Gizzida genetic material. They've found a way to spread the genetic material through the air."

A few sharp cries and murmurs rippled through the survivors.

Arden grabbed Dom's hand.

Holmes held up a palm. "We all know they have a larger bomb. From our questioning, combined with intel from other bases, we now know that there are *three* bombs."

Arden's chest tightened. *Three.*

"Also, from what we've learned, they need to be detonated together," Holmes added.

Now rumbles filled the room, coming mostly from the soldiers.

"Where are the other two?" Marcus asked.

"We don't know yet," the general answered.

More muttering.

"We're all going to die," someone called out.

"We don't know that." The general's voice was firm. "From day one, we've been outnumbered and outgunned. But here we are, two years later, alive, and fighting back. Through our sheer grit, persistence, and resilience, we're still here. We've suffered losses, terrible losses, but we cling to hope. Other bases around the world are doing the same. We will *not* give up."

Around the room, Arden watched people stand a little straighter, their faces filled with determination. Adam Holmes had the innate ability to inspire.

"All the squads will be tasked to find these bombs," Holmes said. "All our Enclave support teams will be working to find ways to destroy the bombs. We will *not* go down without a fight. We will stand together, no matter what happens."

Cheers exploded around the room.

The general nodded. "All squads, please report to the Command Center."

Dom turned to Arden. "I need to go."

"Me too." She swallowed. "Dom..." She wasn't sure what to say, but she wanted to say something.

He touched her jaw. "I won't let the Gizzida turn us into scaly aliens."

She smiled. "Are you going to stop them all by yourself?"

"No. We'll all need to work together. But I won't stop fighting." He stroked the underside of her jaw, making her tremble. "I will not let this soft skin be sullied by the Gizzida."

His thumb brushed her lips, and then he turned and left, pushing through the crowd.

DOM STRODE toward the small conference room assigned to the berserkers.

He paused as he eyed the sketch taped on the door. It showed a muscle-bound, bearded berserker, with a tall, female soldier beside him, threatening to hit him with a frypan.

His lips quirked and he stepped into the room.

"Nice of you to show up, Santora," Levi called out.

Tane nodded at him.

Hemi pointed. "You see that picture?" Hemi grinned.

"Gotta make a copy for Cam. Wish I knew who our mystery artist was."

Griff straightened, his brow creasing. "You sleep in those clothes, Santora?"

Spotting a pot of coffee on the side table, Dom stayed quiet and focused on pouring himself a mug. When he turned, he saw the speculation in his friend's eyes.

"Listen up," Tane said. "We got our assignment."

"Yeah, we need to save the world," Levi said.

"Fuck yeah," Hemi added. "I got a gorgeous woman, and I want to still be sleeping beside her when we're both old, gray, and wrinkly."

For a second, Dom imagined Arden as an elegant, silver-haired woman. She'd be just as beautiful, just as tempting. He knew he'd still want her, however old they were.

"I've seen your ass, Rahia." Levi winked. "You aren't far away from old, gray, and wrinkly."

Hemi shot the man the finger.

Tane ignored the banter. "There are three bombs. Our squad has been tasked with focusing on searching for the large octagon bomb that we saw in Katoomba."

"What about the other two bombs?" Ash asked. "Are they even in Australia?"

"We don't know yet. Other teams are working on locating them, and the general is liaising with the other bases around the world. We'll find 'em."

"So, what's our plan?" Levi asked.

Tane waved at the portable comps resting on the table. "We'll start by searching drone footage."

Groans filled the room. Dom knew how everyone

felt. They were soldiers, men of action, and sitting at computer screens for hours on end was not their idea of fun.

Tane held up a hand. "If we can narrow down some particular search areas, we'll do some recon missions into the mountains." He raised a dark brow. "Recon only. We do not engage the aliens. The bomb is our priority."

The grumbles settled down. The berserkers poured more coffee and got to work. Soon, they were all sitting, searching the footage.

Dom combed through footage from the Gizzida graveyard at Lake Lyell. Memories of the suckers made his lip curl.

"So, is no one going to mention that Dom is wearing last night's clothes?" Hemi said.

Dom raised his head. Hemi was leaning back in his chair, his boots resting on the table.

Griff nodded. "I knocked on his door this morning before Holmes' meeting. He wasn't in."

"So, whose bed did you sleep in, Santora?" Levi asked.

"No one's." It wasn't exactly a lie.

"Wherever you were, I think you were wrapped up with some pretty, young thing." Hemi gave him a knowing wink.

"What will it take for you to drop this?" Dom asked.

"I'm not open to bribes," Hemi lied. "Take your teasing like a man. You guys gave me hell when I was courting Cam."

"Courting?" Levi broke out in laughter.

"Hey, I won her over."

"It took you months," Ash said. "Most of the time, you just drove her crazy."

Hemi grinned unrepentantly. "She still fell head over heels for me. Now—" his gaze locked on Dom "—I want details, my man."

Dom looked back at the comp screen. "I worked for the Mafia. There's nothing you can do to me that'll make me talk."

Hemi let out a sigh. "Damn, you're probably right."

There were good-natured laughs all around, and finally they all got back to work.

But a minute later, Griff leaned in close. "You be careful with her. She's been through a lot. She and Indy are close."

Dom looked at his friend, unsurprised that the former cop had worked it out. "Does Indy—?"

Griff shook his head. "But it won't take my girl long to connect the dots, and I won't lie to her."

"Arden's tougher than she looks," Dom murmured.

Griff gave him a faint smile. "Women always are."

"I'd die for her."

Griff blinked. "Shit, Dom. I didn't realize it was that serious."

"I should never have gone near her, but I wouldn't have without it being serious. I've watched her for a long time."

Griff leaned back in his chair.

"I want to protect her from everything," Dom said. "I want to make her happy, give her pleasure, see her smile."

"That's good. You both deserve it."

Dom shook his head. "I should stay away from her."

Griff cursed. "Why?"

"You know better than anyone what I am." Griff had been a cop once.

Griff gripped Dom's shoulder. "Yeah, I do. You are a man who was born into a shitty life. A man who survived the best he could, and then found a way out. You're a man who fights to protect, who risks his life for others. You're also a good friend and a good man."

Blinking, Dom stared at his friend's face, not quite believing what he'd said. He realized that Griff was pissed. For him.

A strange sensation moved through Dom, and he pulled in a breath. "I—"

"I'm not finished," Griff said. "It's time you quit using your past like a barrier between you and life."

Dom blinked again. "You finished now?"

"Yep, so get back to work." Griff swiped at his comp screen. "We have a bomb to find."

CHAPTER NINE

A rden looked at the footage. *Again*. She rubbed her blurry eyes.

The rest of her squad had gone to bed. As he'd left to find his partner Avery, Roth had threatened Arden with bodily harm if she didn't take a break and get some rest.

But she needed to stay. She needed to keep working. She *needed* to help.

Those poor kids... Arden sat back in a chair and stretched her stiff neck. She knew her emotions were mixed up with the loss of Beth and Emmett. She was okay with that. She was using it to fuel her need to take the Gizzida down.

She wished for the millionth time that she had a photo of Jason and her kids. In those early days, it had tortured her that she had nothing of theirs to hold on to. But now, she realized she had all the important things. Every time she closed her eyes, it was easy to remember Jason bending her over his arm for a kiss, and the snuggles, the giggles, the endless stories her kids would tell her. It was the small things she kept locked in her heart. Jason making his world-famous, homemade pizza, Emmett's bright coloring, Beth's hard hugs. Her husband had been a wonderful father, and her kids had always known they were loved.

Arden opened her eyes, staring blankly at the drone footage on the screen. For her family, for those kids at Mount Wilson, for the survivors at the Enclave, and dammit, for herself, she was going to find this damn bomb.

She wanted to live.

Memories of her hands on Dom, her mouth on him… Arden shivered. She wanted more.

Shaking her head, she concentrated on the screen again.

She'd been over the footage of the town over and over, but she forced herself to study every detail—the bodies, the scales, the claws, the mutations. Her hands clamped onto the edge of the conference room table and she breathed in deeply.

They *would* find this bomb. She wouldn't let the aliens take any more than they already had.

Then she tilted her head, staring at an image of the remnants of the detonated test bomb.

What was that? There was something in the shadows of one of the drag marks gouged into the mud.

Tapping the screen with a frown, she zoomed in on the image.

There. There were lots of deep tracks in the mud from where the Gizzida had dragged the bomb into place.

And in one track, hidden in the shadows, she saw a faint neon glow.

Even zoomed in, she couldn't quite tell what it was. It looked like a strand of lights.

What was it?

"*Bella?*"

His deep voice shivered through her and she looked over her shoulder.

Dom stood in the doorway, wearing his black, carbon-fiber armor, with his carbine slung on one shoulder

"You should be in bed," he said.

"I wanted to look at a few more images."

He walked inside, stopping beside her chair. His gloved fingers brushed her cheek. "You look tired."

She nodded. "You have patrol?"

"I took a shift from Morales from Squad Eight."

She noticed that he was always taking extra shifts, especially from the married or partnered-up soldiers. "I heard his foster son has been sick. You need to rest, too."

Unsurprisingly, he ignored her comment and glanced at her computer screen. "Any luck?"

She shook her head, frustration skating on her nerves. "Not really."

"Maybe you need fresh eyes. You'll do better after some sleep."

Arden nodded again, but she felt the ticking clock. "They could detonate that bomb at any time, Dom."

"We don't know that." He rubbed his thumb across her lips. "Rest now. I'll check on you when I get back from patrol."

Warmth bloomed inside her. It had been a long time since she'd had someone to check on her. "Okay."

His dark gaze narrowed on her. "You should tell me to stay away."

Arden lifted her chin. "It's my choice who I spend time with. And you're the first choice I've made in a long time."

He stared at her, dark eyes unreadable.

"I want to touch you again," she murmured. "Taste you again."

He sucked in a breath. "Code me into the lock on your door. Now, go."

She stood and he ushered her out of the conference room and through the Command Center. As she walked down the hallway, she could feel him watching her.

She glanced back over her shoulder. He stood there, dark and deadly. He lifted his chin, a chunk of thick, black hair falling over his forehead. Then she blinked, and he was gone.

Back in her quarters, Arden quickly showered and changed. As she dropped onto her bed, she was sure she'd toss and turn, worried about the bomb.

Instead, her thoughts were of touching Dom, stroking bronze skin. She dozed off, thinking of him, and dropped into a deep, dreamless sleep.

Arden jerked awake, feeling lips on her collarbone in a gentle, teasing caress.

His scent—soap and freshly-showered skin—washed over her. Desire coiled in her belly and she moaned.

As a strong hand cupped one of her breasts, she shook off the last remnants of sleep. Faint light was spilling from a lamp on the other side of the room. She pulled in a sharp breath, drawing more of Dom's scent into her senses.

Liquid heat ran through her body. She lifted a hand, touching damp hair. His lips moved to her neck, teeth and stubble scraping over her skin. She arched into him, and a strong hand moved down, then pushed the hem of her sleep shirt up.

He pushed it over her belly, over her breasts. Then he lowered his dark head.

"Oh." It felt so good. As his tongue moved over her skin, she looked down. Her belly jumped. The sight of that dark head nestled between her breasts was so sexy.

He tugged on one of her nipples, and she couldn't hold back her moan. He took his time, exploring, tasting, plumping her breasts together with his hands as he sucked and licked them.

Then his head moved lower. His lips traveled across her belly.

"So much beauty," he murmured against her skin.

He glanced up at her and her breath caught. This man looked at her like she was precious. Like he couldn't quite believe she was real.

No one had ever looked at her like that before.

He pushed her thighs apart and moved lower. Anticipation and nerves made her jumpy, like she was going to slip out of her skin.

Then his mouth was on her.

"Dom!" Arden pushed her hips against that clever mouth. His tongue stabbed inside her. Desire spilled through her—hot and demanding—making it hard to breathe.

"I love your taste," he said. "I'm drunk on you, Arden."

Then he didn't say anything else, just kept torturing her with his mouth.

Her last shred of control slipped. She tried to say something, but the pleasure was too big. As sensation crashed over her, her scream echoed in the shadows.

DOM LIFTED HIS HEAD, desire pumping through him.

He was usually always intensely aware of his surroundings. He'd grown up knowing he had to always watch his back.

But with Arden, his focus was only on her.

Aliens could storm the room and he wouldn't notice. And the way she was looking at him right now...

There was need and want mixed in her beautiful, violet-blue eyes. She shifted, pushing herself upright, and jumped on him.

Dom grunted, catching her. Her mouth collided with his, and the kiss was wild, hungry. She straddled him, and he slid one hand into her silky hair. He moved his other hand down to cup her ass.

"*Bella.*"

"I want you, Dom. Now. Inside me, please."

He'd never make his woman beg. Whatever she

needed, he'd give it to her. He yanked the loose shirt she wore over her head. Their eyes locked.

Dom moved one hand between their bodies. Her hips shifted and when his fingers brushed her belly, he felt her suck in a breath.

"I have a contraceptive implant," she panted.

He gripped the base of his throbbing cock and she lifted her hips. The swollen head of him rubbed against her, where she was slick and warm. She bit down on her bottom lip. She shifted again, and his cock lodged against the folds between her legs.

She gasped, he hissed.

Then, with a primal urgency, she gripped his shoulders and lowered herself down.

Intense pleasure. His cock slid inside her and he felt her body give, taking him in. He watched her face, the emotions that flowed through her eyes, the need stamped on her delicate features.

"Dom—"

"Take me, *bella*," he said between gritted teeth.

He saw a flicker of pain on her face, and stilled. He knew it had been a long time for her. But her fingers dug into his skin, and she kept lowering her hips. Determination glinted on her face.

"*Bella*, take your time—"

"No." She kept pushing down. "It stings a little." She made a small, husky sound. "You stretch me."

He growled, his entire body shaking. He wanted to move, to shove completely inside her. To possess.

But he stayed still and let her lead.

Then, finally, he was lodged deep inside. He groaned.

She cupped his cheeks. "It feels so good."

"*Bella*." He kissed her.

She started to rise and fall. As she found her rhythm, her face flushed, and he'd never seen her look more beautiful.

Arden started to move faster, husky sounds coming from her throat. She was taking her pleasure, riding him, using him. And he loved it.

"Yes, Arden."

"Oh, God, Dom!"

He moved his hand between their surging bodies and touched her clit. He thumbed it, rolling it between his fingers.

Her movements turned jerky. "I...oh, oh..."

He gripped her hip with his free hand, keeping her moving. His cock felt ready to burst.

Suddenly, she exploded, her release coming fast and hard. She cried out.

Dom's entire body was on fire. As her body clamped down on his, rippling around his hard cock, he shifted. He shoved her onto her back on the bed.

He felt possessed. He drove into her. Her nails dug into his shoulders.

"Take what you need, my knight."

Her husky murmur made him growl. He thrust inside her over and over. It wasn't gentle or slow, and he needed more. He hitched one slim leg up around his hip, giving him deeper access.

Fast and hard, he hammered inside her. With each thrust, a grunt was torn from him. He wanted to mark her, possess her. He felt like a beast in rut.

Arden moaned beneath him, her arms and legs clinging to him. "Dom!"

"Mine, *bella*." It was a deep, barely intelligible growl.

"Yes!"

And with that final word, Dom's release roared through him. He came, his back arching as he thrust to the root, and he groaned through his orgasm.

CHAPTER TEN

A rden pressed her hands to the tiles in her shower. "I can't hold on," she panted.

"Don't come," Dom growled from behind her.

His thick cock was thrusting inside her, his hands clamped on her hips. She pressed her palms harder against the tiles, trying to stop from splintering apart.

Then he covered her body with his, his chest pressed to her back. His teeth bit into her shoulder, and she moaned.

There was too much sensation. She was sensitive and swollen between her legs, and that made his cock feel even bigger. The warm water was rushing over her, his hard body pressed against hers, his stubble rasping on her skin. It was all too much, too good, and she didn't want it to stop.

She felt fingers slide over her hip and down between her legs. His thrusts increased and his thumb brushed her clit.

"Now get there," he ordered.

He was being rough with her. He didn't treat her like glass, or like she was something broken. Her release hit in a blinding rush and her cries echoed off the tiles.

Dom thrust again and stayed lodged deep. He groaned, his big body shaking.

In the aftermath, they both held each other under the warm pulse of the shower. It took a while, but finally Arden's heartbeat slowed and her breathing evened out. As he soaped them up, she made him turn, and she finally indulged herself tracing his knife tattoo.

"I like this," she said.

"I got it a few years ago. Had the artist sketch up the design."

"It's perfect for you."

He worked shampoo into her hair, massaging her scalp, and she made a moaning sound.

"That's two nights I've spent in your arms," he murmured.

She made a humming sound, nuzzling her face against his chest. One of his hands was resting on her belly, and she liked the way his skin was shades darker than hers.

"I've never slept overnight with a woman before."

Arden stilled and looked up at his face. "Never?"

"Never. I never wanted to and never trusted anyone enough."

He reached past her and turned off the water. He gently pushed her out of the shower stall, and then wrapped a towel around her. She liked the way he looked after her.

He tied a towel around his waist. "My mother was a Mafia prostitute."

His words made Arden freeze.

"She worked for Salvatore Denaro. He was the head of the Ndrangheta." He paused. "One of the largest Mafia groups in Europe. My mother was passed around his men. I have no idea who my father was."

Dom grabbed Arden's hand and pulled her out into her quarters. Processing his words took a second, but it was the tone of his voice that got to her. So blank, so empty.

She sat down on the edge of the bed, hitching her towel up higher. "That had to be tough."

He sank into an armchair nearby, resting his hands between his knees.

"She died of a drug overdose when I was seven."

Sympathy for a tiny, neglected boy rushed through Arden.

"The Ndrangheta controlled the largest supply of cocaine in Europe, and a few decades ago, they'd moved into Zenith."

Arden recognized the name of the designer drug. It had become popular about fifty years ago.

"After my mother died, Salvatore kept me around." Dom sat still and straight. "I became his errand boy. He gave me a bunk in the back room of one of his warehouses." Dom paused. "When I was old enough, he trained me to fight. Turned out I was good with knives. I had to fight for my food."

A tremor went through Arden. She wanted to touch him but she wasn't sure he'd welcome it. She tucked a strand of wet hair behind her ear. "That's cruel. And it's no life for a child."

"I owed him."

No, screw this. She moved over to Dom, kneeling at his feet. She gripped his leg. "You didn't owe him anything. He was a criminal."

Dom didn't say anything, and Arden understood. It was all he'd ever known. Salvatore was the closest thing he'd had to a father, to family. The man had used him, and the small acts of kindness had seemed like something good.

"When I got older, I became his enforcer." Now Dom's tone was downright cold. "I killed for him."

Heart aching, she rose up, crawling into his lap. "You think that changes how I feel about you? You were a child, Dom. An abused one with very few options."

"But then I became an adult, Arden."

She tilted her head. "And how did you end up here? At Blue Mountain Base, and then the Enclave?"

He paused, his dark eyes on her face.

"Well?" she urged.

"I was with Salvatore in Sydney when the aliens came. He had a meeting with some drug suppliers."

"And?"

"During the attack, I..." He looked over her shoulder. "I killed Salvatore and escaped."

"You finally saw a chance, and you took it."

"I'm thirty-five, Arden. I'd been doing his dirty work for a long time."

"Would he ever have let you leave?"

"Never. No one leaves the Ndrangheta. I knew far too much."

Dom was the only person who didn't realize that there was a good man buried inside him. She pressed a palm to his bare chest, right over his beating heart. Then she moved her head and touched her lips to his.

As they kissed, his body relaxed. He pulled her closer. "You are too good for me, Arden."

"Stop saying that. I won't listen to it anymore."

A faint smile touched his lips. "I have to meet my squad."

"I have to go, too. I promised to meet Indy for breakfast."

They kissed again, and then took their time dressing. Arden watched him shrug into his shirt, then run a hand through his thick hair. He probably had no clue how sexy those simple moves were. As she slipped into her own shirt, she realized they were almost behaving like any other normal couple.

Although they were far from normal.

"Good luck with your search today." He ran his finger down her nose.

"You, too. I'm hoping my brain won't leak out my ears from the boredom of searching drone footage."

"I heard Hemi mutter something similar."

With one last kiss, Dom was gone. Without his presence beside her, Arden felt lonely. Then she smiled. She had quite a few pleasant aches, and a few sexy memories, that kept him on her mind.

Shaking her head, she headed for the dining room. When she entered, she spotted Indy at a table, tablet in one hand, and a glass of juice in the other. As Arden approached, her friend looked up with a smile on her face.

Indy's smile froze, then widened. "You got laid."

Arden stumbled to a halt. "What?"

"Soft face, dreamy eyes, relaxed body." Indy smirked and raised a brow. "And stubble burn on your neck."

Automatically, Arden reached up to touch the tender skin on her neck.

Indy lowered her tablet. "I *knew* it. Spill, girl. I want details. It was that teacher who asked you out the other week, right?"

Arden sat and reached over to pour a cup of tea.

"Arden."

She met her friend's gaze. "No, it wasn't Paul. Um, it was Dom."

Indy blinked and her mouth dropped open. "Dom? As in Dominic Santora?"

Arden nodded.

"You got naked with the most dangerous man in the Enclave?"

"There are a lot of dangerous men in the Enclave. You sleep with one of them."

"Yes, but no one radiates that dark intensity that says 'I could kill you in ten seconds' like Dom does."

Arden sipped her drink. "He's not dangerous to me." She smiled, thinking of the way he held her.

"So I see." Indy tilted her head. "Wow. Just give my poor brain a second to process." Indy wagged a finger. "Okay, I'll admit to wondering just how that sexy Italian is between the sheets."

Arden smiled. "Amazing."

Indy grinned. "I am so damn happy for you, Ard. You snagged yourself a sexy berserker."

Then the two of them burst into giggles and it felt so good.

DOM'S CHAIR creaked as he shifted. He was back in a conference room, poring over more footage.

He was trying to focus on the image in front of him, but all he could think about was Arden—the sound she made when he slid inside her, the way her hair smelled, the taste of her skin.

"Dom? Earth to Dom? Hey!"

Dom looked up and saw all of his squad mates staring at him. "What?"

Griff shook his head. "You're a million miles away."

Dom just grunted.

"He needs to get laid, I tell you," Hemi said.

Dom shot Hemi a look. "The only thing I need is to find this bomb. There's no need for you to worry about my sex life, Rahia."

Hemi snorted. "Especially when you don't have one."

Levi set a file down on the table. "We've found dick-all. I say we get back out there. There's nothing in these pictures."

Tane rose and started pacing. "We can't cover the entire Blue Mountains on foot. We need to narrow things down. Where would the Gizzida take this bomb?"

"Somewhere well hidden," Ash suggested. "And they can't have taken it too far, or we'd have noticed."

The team started spitballing, tossing out theories, each one wilder than the next, but slowly, every single idea was discarded.

The fact of the matter was, they didn't have one fucking clue.

The door opened and Indy entered. Their comms officer was juggling a large coffee mug and her portable comp. She moved over and dropped a kiss on Griff's lips before she sat down. Then she looked straight at Dom and smiled at him.

Shit. She knew.

She winked at him.

As his team continued to brainstorm, Dom focused back on the discussion. Indy joined in, offering her own theories and opinions.

"We've got nothing." Tane pressed his hands to the table. Frustration throbbed off him.

Then the door flew open.

"Lunch," the redhead in the doorway called out.

"Hey, Spitfire." Levi grinned at his woman.

Chrissy smiled as she carried a large box. She had some grease stains on her tank top, no doubt from her maintenance job. A cute blonde wearing glasses appeared beside her, carrying some drinks.

Chrissy dropped the box of sandwiches on the table and sauntered over to Levi. The man pulled her into his lap and kissed her like there was no one else in the room. Marin Mitchell from the tech team shot a wide-eyed smile at Ash, her blonde curls bouncing. The tattooed berserker rose, pulling her into his arms.

Dom watched the men's faces light up.

He could have that. He could have that with Arden. Someone who was solely his, for the first time ever in his entire life. Someone who made crawling through the darkness worth it.

As his team mates reached for the sandwiches, Dom realized that he finally had something worth fighting for.

But before he and Arden had a future, he first had to protect her and ensure their survival.

"How's the search going?" Chrissy asked.

Levi groaned. "Don't ask. If I have to look at more drone footage, I'm going to let the Gizzida kill me."

Sitting beside Ash, Marin leaned forward, nibbling on a salad. "The tech team is doing more tests on the samples you guys brought back from the town." Her shoulders slumped. "But nothing new so far."

"How are the other squads doing?" Tane asked.

Marin pulled a face. "Same as you guys. Slow and frustrated." She nibbled on some lettuce. "Holmes is working with the other bases. He's talking to Groom Lake right now. Everyone knows we have to find the other two bombs."

A sour mood fell over the room and everyone picked at their food.

When the door opened again, Dom leaned back in his chair and glanced over. Arden rushed in, her hair mussed.

"Ard?" Indy said.

Dom leaped to his feet. Arden's gaze hit him and she circled the table, making a beeline straight to him.

"I found something!" She was breathless. "The rest of my squad has gone to lunch, but I had to tell somebody."

"Calm down, *bella*."

She slapped a hand to his chest. "I think I know where the bomb might be." She went up on her toes, pressing her mouth to his.

It was Arden, so naturally, Dom's brain short-circuited. He wrapped an arm around her and kissed her back.

He sensed the mood in the room change. He pulled her close to his side and looked up.

Griff was flat-out grinning. Ash, Levi, and Tane were looking on with raised eyebrows. Chrissy was elbowing Marin, Indy looked smug, and Hemi appeared shocked.

"What the fuck, Santora?" Hemi said. "You've been holding out on us."

Arden blinked, as though she was suddenly realizing that there were other people in the room.

"Ah..." Pink filled her cheeks.

Dom just held her tighter. "Tell us what you found, *bella*."

"This." She slapped the printout she was holding onto the table. Everyone rose, leaning over to look at it.

It was an image. Dom recognized the remnants of the test bomb, sitting among a bunch of track marks in the mud.

"Okay." Tane frowned. "The test bomb. We've all seen it."

"Not the bomb. *Here.*" Arden pointed to a smudge on the image.

Dom frowned. There was a faint smear of blue-green color in one of the track marks.

Everyone traded confused looks.

"We need more, Arden," Dom said.

"The blue-green mark. Here, I enlarged it." She set another picture down on the table.

There was some more detail to it now. Dom's frown deepened. It wasn't really clear, but it looked like a string of pearls.

"What is it?" Indy asked.

"It's a glow worm larva," Arden said.

Glow worms? That didn't mean much to Dom.

Hemi grunted. "Tane, remember that family vacation?"

Tane nodded. "Back in New Zealand. Our parents took us on a boat tour through Waitomo Caves when we were kids."

"The glow worms were amazing," Hemi said. "Like stars."

"Glow worms are a common name for a few different types of insect larvae that glow through bioluminescence," Arden said.

"I'm guessing the bomb isn't in a cave in New Zealand," Indy said.

"Newnes Plateau." Arden practically bounced on her feet. "There's a famous glow worm tunnel in the Blue Mountains. It's an old, abandoned train tunnel that is filled with glow worm larvae. They used to do tours of it, pre-invasion."

Dom stiffened. Now it clicked. "This larva got transferred to Mount Wilson when they moved the test bomb."

She nodded. "That's my theory. Yes."

Tane stood. "And maybe this tunnel is where they're keeping the main bomb."

Arden nodded again.

Indy tapped on her comp screen, pulling up a map.

"Here. The tunnel isn't far from Mount Wilson! About thirty kilometers as the crow flies."

Dom pulled Arden up on her toes. "Nice work, *bella*."

"Thanks."

Tane straightened. "This is great, Arden." He looked around the room. "I'll inform the general. I want all of you ready to move."

"Thank fuck for that," Levi said.

CHAPTER ELEVEN

Arden tried not to fidget as she stood in the busy Command Center with Indy, and Elle Steele from Hell Squad, flanking her.

General Holmes came out of the door leading to one of the conference rooms. He strode to the front of the crowd and Arden thought he looked stressed. His shirt was rumpled, and he looked like he'd been running his hands through his silver-tinged, dark hair.

She'd shared her discovery about the glow worm larvae with him. He'd been about to go back into a call with the Groom Lake base.

Holmes straightened and ran his gaze over the assembled squads. "Groom Lake has intel."

The air in the room changed, sharpening. Arden turned her head and glanced at Dom. He gave her a small nod.

Just that small move eased some of the tension in her chest.

"They interrogated a Gizzida prisoner," the general said. "A scientist." He took a deep breath. "They've confirmed that there are three bombs. They need to be placed in certain locations around the planet and detonated together."

"Why?" Tane called out.

"Apparently, doing so will amplify their effect...and ensure the entire planet is covered with Gizzida genetic material."

God. Arden's stomach dropped away. This was worse than she'd ever imagined.

"Fuckers," Indy muttered.

"If we can destroy one bomb, that will mitigate the effect," Holmes said. "And give the other bases time to search for the other two bombs."

The soldiers in the room shifted restlessly. Tane stood with his hands on his hips, staring at the ground. Marcus looked like he wanted to punch something. Roth looked angry.

"From what the scientist shared, one of the bombs is in the North American region. Groom Lake is working to track it down. Nothing concrete yet."

"And the other?" Marcus asked.

Holmes lifted one shoulder and blew out a breath. "No sign of it yet. The Gizzida scientist didn't know where it was."

"So, we need to destroy the bomb we know is here," Tane confirmed.

The general nodded.

"How?" Hemi asked. "If we blow it up, it's gonna spread alien DNA all over the place."

Noah stepped forward. "My team's best guess is that we should drain the liquid out of the bomb and destroy the detonating mechanism."

Marcus crossed his arms over his chest. "But the aliens can remake the bomb, right? Fill it back up again."

Noah nodded. "Sure, they could. But that will take time. Right now, we need time to find the other two bombs and find a more decisive solution for destroying them."

"And we now have a location of where our bomb is?" Marcus asked.

The general turned his blue gaze to Arden. He waved her forward.

Clearing her throat, Arden addressed the crowd. "I found glow worm larva in the footage from Mount Wilson." The picture flashed up on the screen. "There's a well-known glow worm tunnel close by."

More pictures appeared, these ones from the archives. They showed the amazing beauty of the glow worm tunnel. The glow worm larvae lit up the roof of the tunnel like stars scattered through the night sky.

"I don't know for certain that the bomb itself is there," Arden continued. "But it was likely that the test bomb was."

"Tane," Holmes said. "I'm tasking this to your squad."

Tane nodded, one dreadlock falling over his broad shoulder.

"Hell Squad and Squad Nine," Holmes continued. "You're on standby as their back-up."

"General." A soft, female voice cut through the room. "I'd like to go on the mission."

Arden turned and spotted Selena stepping through the crowd. From nearby, Tane growled.

The general looked at the alien woman for a second. He glanced at Tane, before he looked back at Selena. "Your skills would be welcomed, Selena. We need to throw whatever we have at destroying this bomb."

"This is my home, too." Her large, green eyes flickered to Tane for a brief second. "I'll fight to protect it."

Arden shifted a little. "I'd like to go as well. With the combat drone—"

Dom stepped forward, two menacing steps. "Arden."

"This is also my fight," she said. "I want to help."

Dom ground his teeth together, then cursed in Italian.

"Welcome to my fucking club," Tane muttered to Dom.

Noah cleared his throat. "I've equipped Arden's combat drone with our new cineole weapons."

"You've finished testing them?" Holmes asked.

The head of the tech team nodded. "We've been running non-stop tests. We know the cineole breaks down the raptor's cellular structure with enough exposure. My team has amplified the affects as much as we can. It will certainly help weaken them."

Excited whispers rippled through the soldiers.

They'd known for a long time that the raptors were affected by the trees on Earth. Now they had a chance to use it to the benefit of all humans. Maybe these weapons could help turn the tide of the fight.

Noah looked at Squad Three. "I'd be happy to add some cineole to your weapons."

The berserkers all nodded.

"If it makes them bleed, then bring it," Hemi said.

Tane was looking up at the screen. "The trees are too thick around the glow worm tunnel entrance to land the Hawks."

Indy nodded and tapped on a comp. "I agree. I suggest you ride up the track that leads to the entrance on your bikes." She tapped again. "From here."

A map flashed on the screen, a glowing dot appearing.

Tane nodded.

"Okay, everyone knows their jobs." Holmes scanned the room. "There's a lot riding on this mission." He gave a faint smile. "And I know the berserkers will make a mess and make the Gizzida sorry they tangled with us."

"Hell yeah!" Hemi shouted.

"Hey, that's our battle cry," Shaw from Hell Squad said. "Get your own."

Arden looked at Dom.

He shot her a molten glare before he turned and stalked out. Her chest hitched.

"Uh-oh," Indy murmured. "Trouble in paradise."

Arden sighed. "I have to go on this mission, Indy."

"I know. He knows, too, but these alpha males have this built-in need to keep their women safe." Indy smiled. "Some latent caveman gene. He'll come around."

Arden swallowed. She hoped so.

DOM WAS BARELY able to control his anger. He

pulled his knives out of his locker, shoving them into the sheaths on his belt.

He'd already been forced to take Arden out in the field once. He did not want to do it again.

All around him in the locker room, his squad was getting ready for the mission. Dom was already in his armor, but the others were in various states of undress.

Nearby, Levi was still naked and taking his time. The man took forever to get dressed. Hemi was still shirtless, joking around with Ash and trying to break the tension in the room.

Suddenly, the door opened, and Arden stepped inside.

Dom stiffened. Her gaze skated around the room, danced over Levi and Hemi, before zooming straight to Dom. Her cheeks were pink.

He strode toward her, grabbed her arm, and yanked her out of the room.

"I'm sorry you're angry," she said.

In the hall, Dom let her go and dragged in a breath.

"The last mission went fine," she said. "You and the squad protected me—"

"Since then I've had my cock inside you. I don't want my woman anywhere near the Gizzida, let alone this bomb."

His tone was sharper than his blades.

Arden licked her lips. "I'd love to hide, Dom. A part of me would love to let everyone else do the dirty work, the scary work. But if those bombs go off, they kill us all. I *want* to fight. I want to fight for my dead husband, for my children—" Her chest hitched.

And just like that, Dom's anger broke. He hated seeing her pain and wanted to soothe her. He yanked her in close, pulling her hard against his chest in a tight hug.

Her arms wrapped around him, holding on.

"I want to do it for them, but I also want to do it for us. I want more time with you, Dom."

Damn. She knew exactly how to batter down every one of his defenses. "Arden..."

She looked up at him. "So, I'm your woman?"

"*Si.*"

She smiled. "Good. And that means you're my man."

He yanked her up on her toes, pressing his mouth to hers. He thrust his tongue inside, kissing her deeply.

When they broke apart, she touched her fingers to her swollen lips. "You make me so dizzy."

"And you touch places inside me that no one has ever touched before."

Warmth moved over her face. "Dom."

He released a breath. "We have a mission to get ready for."

She nodded, setting her shoulders back. "I need to get into my armor and get the combat drone from Noah."

Dom fiddled with the silk of her hair. "I'll see you at the Hawk."

He stood in the corridor and watched her walk away. Whatever he had to do, he'd keep her safe. He'd open a vein for her, kill for her, die for her.

He finished getting prepped, and soon was standing with his squad beside the Hawk. Levi and Ash started loading up the berserkers' heavily armored motorcycles into the back of the Hawk.

Selena arrived next. The slender woman was in armor, her silver-white hair braided.

Dom glanced at Tane. His leader was silent, but a muscle was ticking in the man's jaw.

"You follow my orders," Tane barked at Selena.

Her chin lifted. "I'll do what the mission requires."

Tane's eyes narrowed and Dom bit his tongue. It hadn't escaped any of them that the woman hadn't exactly agreed to obey.

Then Arden appeared. As she walked into the hangar, her gaze met Dom's. She smiled at him. She held the large combat drone in one hand and he moved over to take it from her. The damn thing was heavy.

"Ready?" he asked.

"I'm ready."

"All right." Tane's deep voice reverberated around them. "Let's go destroy a bomb."

CHAPTER TWELVE

A rden's belly was jumping all over the place, like it
was filled with twisting snakes.

She sat in the Hawk, trying to keep her breathing
steady. A jumble of voices murmured around her and
Dom was a solid presence sitting beside her. She was glad
he was with her.

She knew just how important—and dangerous—this
mission was.

After some time, the quadcopter began to descend,
and she knew that they were at the drop site.

The berserkers all rose, looking calm and focused.
She scanned them one by one. So tough, so lethal. Each
of them, regardless of their past lives, had been on so
many missions like this, ready to fight, defend, and
protect.

Tane, his dreadlocks pulled back at the base of his
neck, opened the side door. His dark gaze caught hers, his
face so emotionless. He gave her a brief nod.

Then Dom's fingers curled around her arm. She looked at him and saw the same steady determination.

These men wouldn't let fear stop them. They'd fight —for her, for the others at the Enclave, for a chance at life.

And Arden would do the same.

She let Dom help her up and reached down to grab the combat drone off an empty seat. Outside, she gazed at all the trees, pulling in the green scent of the forest. A wide, muddy track speared away to the north. A second Hawk swept into view above them, its illusion system flickering off to reveal its dull, gray body. She spotted Finn Erickson, their best Hawk pilot, in the cockpit. He flicked two fingers at them.

Selena joined Arden. The alien woman somehow looked nervous and calm all at once.

"Okay?" Arden asked.

"I was going to ask you the same thing."

"I'll be happier once this is over."

Together, they watched the berserkers set up two small ramps and roll their monstrous bikes off the Hawks. As the men each claimed their bikes, she watched them start to mount up. They all suited their machines—big, rugged, unique.

Tane turned to Selena and raised a hand. He curled a finger at her. Selena hesitated for a second, then walked over. Gingerly, the alien woman climbed on behind the squad leader.

Arden turned, pressing the buttons on the drone to activate it. With a beep, it rose up in the air, hovering above her.

Nearby, Dom swung a muscled leg over his bike and settled on the seat. She saw him start the silent, thermonuclear engine.

"Have you been on a bike before?" he asked.

She shook her head.

He held out a hand to her and she took it. She trusted this man with everything—her body, her battered soul, her dented heart. She swung on behind him. He pulled her arms around his middle, and she held on tight.

"Don't let go," he warned her.

She nestled into him, their bodies pressed together. For a brief second, she hated the carbon fiber between them. They were about to head into a dangerous situation, deep in alien territory, but strangely, Arden felt safe. Dom made her feel safe, but it was more than that. Arden felt stronger, like she could do her part.

Her kids would be proud of her. Jason would call her badass.

"No raptors on screen, Tane." Indy's calm voice in their earpieces.

"Acknowledged. We're heading up the track now." Tane's bike shot forward, Hemi following.

Dom took off, and Arden clenched her fingers harder around his stomach.

He followed the others and they moved down the overgrown track. The trees grew thick around them, and pretty ferns grew in profusion as well.

She could easily imagine the tourists trekking down this path, excited to be heading to see the glow worm tunnel. The echoes of old voices rang in her ears.

The Gizzida had stolen so much. Taken what wasn't

theirs.

Today, that ended.

Arden looked all around at the other berserkers. The bikes were silent, but they still looked badass.

They bumped along the rutted track, taking the turns and curves. Dom dodged some heavy potholes and track marks that looked quite new. Her stomach tightened. They were in the right place.

"You guys should be at the tunnel entrance." Indy's voice over the comm line.

Arden felt the bike slow beneath her. She leaned around Dom and looked ahead.

The entrance to the tunnel loomed before them.

It was a large, oval shape, with ferns hanging down all around it. The ground in front of it was disturbed, with deep, rutted marks.

Her throat thickened. The aliens had been here.

Tane lifted his hand, and everyone pulled the bikes to a stop. The berserkers cut the engines, then rolled the bikes off to the side of the track.

As everyone dismounted, Arden checked the drone. It hovered silently in the air nearby, already starting to scan and record the area. Around her, the berserkers moved into position, lifting their carbines.

"I'm ready to blow up some alien shit," Hemi muttered.

Arden looked at Dom, so still and composed. His gloved hands were wrapped around his weapon, his knives ready and sheathed on his belt.

"Let's move." Tane jerked his head.

As one, they moved toward the tunnel entrance. Arden's heart beat hard and loudly in her ears.

They stepped inside the darkness and into a fairytale.

Arden couldn't hold back a gasp. She arched her head, looking at the sprinkle of color along the roof of the tunnel. The glow worms looked like stars. Nearby, she saw Selena staring in wonder, her face alight.

"Keep quiet," Tane murmured. "We don't want to announce to the aliens that we're here. Indy, we're heading deeper into the tunnel."

Indy's garbled, distorted voice came over the comm.

Tane's lips pressed into a hard line. "Damn. We're losing comms in the tunnel."

They marched deeper into the glow worm tunnel.

Arden tried not to trip, but the glow worms didn't give off much light. Just enough to make out the shadows of the others.

They kept moving, and she couldn't begin to guess how far they'd gone. Ahead, she sensed the tunnel widening out.

The drone moved in front of her, and she knew it was scanning. She had a tiny screen attached to her wrist, the screen's brightness down as low as possible. She glanced at it, and saw no sound, no heat signatures.

"I can't see a fucking thing," Hemi muttered.

"Do we risk flashlights?" Ash asked.

"Stop," Tane murmured in their earpieces.

They all stopped, except for Selena. She took a few more steps forward. Tane reached for her, but the woman lifted a hand toward the roof. Her fingers uncurled.

All of a sudden, the glow worms flared brightly.

Arden bit her lip, watching as a wash of blue-green light filled the tunnel.

Oh, God. Selena was communicating with the tiny creatures. *Incredible.* The light illuminated the rough-hewn, rock walls and bumpy floor.

And the octagon-shaped bomb resting in the center of the space.

The men all swiveled, aiming their carbines and muttering curses.

Arden's drone beeped softly and she quickly lifted her tablet screen. Her heart leaped into her throat. "I have heat signatures." Her voice was an urgent whisper. "They're flaring to life all over the tunnel."

A deep, inhuman growl echoed through the tunnel, raising the hairs on the back of her neck. She felt the berserkers tense all around her. She lifted her head and watched hellions wink into life in the tunnel.

They had long, canine-like bodies, with spikes along their backs. Drool dripped from their jaws and they had red-glowing bellies filled with poison.

The alien hunting dogs slunk out of the darkness. Somehow, they'd been camouflaged, and her mind turned to the stealth raptor she'd tangled with.

"Arden, get to the bomb," Tane ordered. "Squad Three, let's make a little mess."

"With pleasure," Levi said.

The berserkers opened fire. The laser fire was loud in the enclosed space, lighting up the darkness.

Arden darted to the side, moving along the wall.

She watched the hellions bound toward the berserkers. Her heart was hammering hard and she prayed everyone would be okay. She saw carbine fire hit the lead hellion. Its belly exploded, its body tumbling over and over before it smacked into the ground. The red ooze from its stomach, sizzling as it made contact with the dirt.

As more hellions raced toward the berserkers, growls and snarls filled the air.

"Bring it on, baby." Hemi's cry.

She had to get to the bomb.

Inching farther along the wall, the big, dark shape of the device loomed ahead. She had to cross several meters to get to it.

She lifted her chin. She could do this.

Then suddenly, a hellion leaped in front of her. It lowered its head and snarled.

Oh, shit. Arden froze, just as her drone swung in front of it. She heard a whirr, then the drone sprayed a clear oil at the creature.

The sharp scent of cedar filled the air, and the hellion started snarling wildly. It shook its head frantically for a moment, before it slunk away and disappeared.

She blew out a breath. *Thanks, Noah.*

Arden set her shoulders back. Time to destroy the bomb.

DOM THREW A GRENADE. It arced through the air and landed in a clump of hellions.

One, two, three. It exploded, spraying cedar oil all over the creatures. They started shaking their heads and snarling.

No, you don't like that, do you? Carbine fire was brighter than the glow worms above, lighting up the tunnel.

Nearby, Hemi roared, firing oil from the end of his carbine. "Take that, assholes."

The yips and cries of the injured hellions filled the space.

Dom kept firing, but lifted his head, searching for Arden. He saw her close to the far wall. He watched her drone drive off a hellion.

His gut clenched. He hated that she was here, in danger. The need to protect her was so strong it damn near strangled him.

She darted forward, running closer to the bomb.

So brave—beautiful and elegant, but steel and iron beneath her soft skin. She was a true survivor.

Suddenly, Griff cursed savagely. Dom spun just in time to see Griff trip over the rough ground. Sensing a weakness, a hellion leaped into the air, claws slashing. It pounced on Griff.

Dom yanked a knife out and threw it. It hit the hellion in the face, and the alien dog let out one yelp. It landed hard beside Griff and toppled over.

Dom slapped his hand against Griff's and yanked his friend up.

"Thanks, man," Griff said.

Together, they both lifted their carbines. They walked forward, firing on the pack of alien dogs.

"Raptors," Tane yelled.

Dom tensed. He scanned the back of the tunnel and spotted them coming out of the shadows on the far side of the bomb.

Cazzo, Arden would be caught between the berserkers and the raptors.

Levi threw a grenade and it arrowed through the air. "Cineole."

The grenade exploded, spewing oil over the alien soldiers. Grunts and guttural shouts filled the air. Dom saw the closest raptor press a claw to its head, blood weeping from its eyes.

Dom checked on Arden again. She was crouched down low, watching the fight. She wasn't at the bomb yet, but she was close.

Her drone was busy firing on the raptors.

The berserkers kept moving forward, kept firing, kept fighting. *They had this.* Dom smiled briefly. Only a few more hellions, and then they could take down the remaining raptors.

Then they could disable the bomb and get the fuck out of here. He could get Arden back to safety.

The ground trembled.

What the hell?

Dom looked at the dirt floor. Something burst out of the ground near his boots. As adrenaline surged through him, he watched a tentacle shoot upward with a spray of dirt. The damn thing was as thick as his waist, and a dark, fleshy gray. It slammed into him and knocked him over.

"Watch out!" he shouted.

Dom hit the dirt and rolled. He sat up, and all around,

he saw the berserkers cursing and dodging. More tentacles were spearing up out of the ground. Another tentacle broke out of the dirt and started coming right at him.

Cazzo. Dom saw the suckers all over the tentacle and he rolled. He whipped his carbine around, firing on the tentacle.

It burst open, goo flying everywhere.

Shit. Damn. Fuck. A rush of realization hit him.

The small suckers they'd seen at Lake Lyell had been *babies.* This was the mama.

He leaped to his feet, firing on any tentacles that he could see.

He heard a woman scream and spun. Arden was surrounded by several tentacles, all of them waving wildly, keeping her caged in.

"*Cazzo.*" Dom aimed and fired.

Her drone joined in and a second later, she darted away from the tentacles.

A larger tentacle speared upright in the center of the tunnel. With a shout, Hemi opened fire on it. But the tentacle swung, slamming right into Hemi. It lifted the man off his feet and threw him into the tunnel wall.

Nearby, several tentacles burst up in front of Selena. Tane fired on them, but two more came up behind her. Selena spun.

"Selena, get out of there!" Tane roared.

She ignored him, crouched, and pressed a hand to the ground.

Dom wasn't sure what she was doing, but the tentacle started waving faster, more frantically.

Then the tentacles closest to the woman burst open, one by one.

Selena smiled and rose.

With terrifying swiftness, another tentacle slithered across the ground, aiming right at Selena. Dom opened his mouth, but before he could warn her, it wrapped around one of her legs and yanked her off the ground.

She hung upside down, struggling to break free.

Tane ran toward her. He leaped over another tentacle, sprinting closer.

More tentacles speared up out of the dirt. Dom turned and fired. Tane would get Selena. Dom had his own woman to keep safe.

Arden was facing two more tentacles. Every time she tried to dodge them, they matched her movements. Beyond the bomb, raptors were firing their poison-filled weapons.

The berserkers kept firing, but more and more tentacles appeared.

One rammed into Levi, its suckers clinging to his armor.

"It burns," Levi yelled. The man yanked out his gladius combat knife and slashed at the tentacle.

Dom kept firing.

He had to get to Arden. He had to help his squad.

He'd had next to nothing his entire life. Now, he had friends—brothers—and he had a woman who was his. He wasn't letting anyone take them from him.

CHAPTER THIRTEEN

Arden darted toward the bomb. Just a few more meters—

A tentacle reared up out of the ground, knocking her back.

She tripped and fell on her ass with a cry. The tentacle with its ugly suckers rushed at her. With a yelp, she rolled out of the way.

Oh, God.

Her heart was pounding, her stomach churning. There were tentacles everywhere and she could hear the grunts of the nearby raptors.

Above her head, the drone's rotors whirred, and the machine started firing. The tentacle whipped around, trying to evade the weapon. The lasers hit their target. The tentacle exploded, and she was splattered with... *Ugh.* Wincing and swiping at her face, she pushed to her knees.

All around her, the berserkers were fighting, tooth

and nail. Ash was dragging Levi away from the mêlée. Hemi was roaring as he fired his weapon. Griff was lobbing several grenades. Tane was a force of nature. With a grim face, he leaped into the air, spraying carbine fire all around.

The squad leader landed, then yanked a grenade off his belt. He tossed it upward.

The weapon exploded, spraying cineole oil everywhere. The tentacles whipped around in a violent frenzy.

Tane kept moving forward, ignoring the tentacles, focused.

And that's when Arden saw Selena.

Oh, no. The woman was held in the air by a tentacle, being whipped around like a broken doll.

As the cineole hit the tentacle, it wiggled faster and shriveled. It dropped Selena.

Tane lunged forward and went down on one knee, catching her against his chest.

Arden swiveled her head and saw Dom whirling and lunging, his knives in his hands. Dark and deadly, he slashed at several tentacles.

A tentacle dropped to the ground, swiping at his boots. He dived over it, rolled, and came up fighting.

Focus, Arden. She turned, her gaze falling on the bomb. She had a job to do. Sucking in a deep breath, she ran.

She jumped over a tentacle, dodged another, then another one slammed into her. *Crap.* She threw herself on the ground, going with the momentum of the blow. The tentacle swept over her, and she rolled across the dirt.

Ouch. She wasn't anywhere as nimble as Dom, but she was alive. Her drone appeared, spraying oil and laser fire around.

Nearby, several tentacles retracted. Arden pushed to her feet. The bomb was *right* there.

She'd taken two steps when she spotted the raptors.

Her heart lodged in her throat. They were walking toward her, large-scaled weapons in their hands. One fired, sending ugly, green poison splattering on the walls. Their eyes were glowing red, like demons in the dark.

Arden ducked around the side of the bomb. She had to get this done...fast.

"Drone, target raptors."

Her drone whirled and fired cineole oil. Arden focused on the black surface of the bomb. It had a matte finish, absorbing the light. She quickly pressed a small targeting patch to the bottom of the device.

She stepped back. "Drone, fire laser cutter."

Her drone moved into position. A small arm swiveled, and then a narrow green laser shot out, piercing into the black metal where she'd applied the target.

She watched, heart pounding. *Come on, come on.*

A hole opened up in the metal and the laser abruptly stopped.

But no fluid came out of the bomb.

What? Frowning, she moved forward, smoothing her hand over the black metal. She circled around it. She couldn't quite see over the top of it since it was too big and closed up. Then she felt a panel depress under her fingers, and she snatched her hand back.

With a click, the top of the octagon bomb started to open, unfurling like a flower.

Arden quickly moved around the side, looking for a way that she could boost herself up and look into the top.

She heard a grunt and spun.

And found herself face-to-face with a raptor.

Her lungs contracted. The alien towered over her, close to seven feet tall. She froze, suddenly unable to breathe.

The raptor's gaze fixated on her. She saw blood oozing from its eyes and ears. It clutched a huge weapon in his claws. Its dark-gray scales looked thick, its chest covered in old scars.

She could swear the raptor was smiling at her, baring sharp teeth.

Suddenly, a burst of fury uncoiled in her belly. These aliens had taken so much from her. Anger flowed through her like a molten river. She charged forward, shoving her hands against the raptor's gut.

It grunted in surprise and Arden quickly pressed one of the target patches onto his scales.

"Fire," she cried out.

The drone fired. As the laser blasts hit the raptor, his body jerked wildly. He collapsed at her feet.

Steeling herself, Arden stepped on top of the dead raptor. She used the added height to peer over inside the bomb.

Her heart dropped. It was *empty*.

She stepped back, her knees unsteady. The bomb was just an empty shell.

She touched her earpiece. "Tane, the bomb is empty. It's a decoy."

"Fuck," came the squad leader's harsh reply across the line.

Arden spun. The tunnel was like a war zone, lit up by the glow worms above and the laser fire below. Raptor poison sprayed the walls and floors, sizzling as it ate into rock and dirt. The sharp scent of cedar and cineole filled the air.

Her gaze fell on Dom. He kicked a raptor, then spun and threw a knife. It lodged in a raptor's chest and the alien threw its head back and roared.

She watched as more raptors converged on him.

Adrenaline surged. For so long she'd been holding back, drowning in her grief. But Dom had woken her up. He made her want to live.

"Drone, target raptors around Dom Santora."

The drone zoomed forward, its weapons humming. It opened fire.

She had taken several steps forward when tentacles erupted out of the ground around Dom.

One slammed into him and he staggered.

No.

Two tentacles wrapped around him and lifted him into the air. One was wrapped around his left leg, and the other around his shoulder and right arm. He jerked, trying to get free.

The tendons in his neck strained, and he let out a shout.

Ice slid into Arden's veins. The tentacles were

pulling him in different directions. Trying to tear him apart.

"Dom!" She broke into a sprint. "Dom!"

———

AGONY RIPPED THROUGH DOM. His bones and joints were being stretched to the breaking point.

He tried to push the pain down. He swiped out with his right arm, trying to cut the tentacles with his knife.

"Dom!" Arden's frantic scream.

"Hang on, Dom!" Griff's shout.

Laser fire roared nearby.

Dom turned his head. He watched Arden's drone whizz past him, firing on the tentacles holding him.

Suddenly, the tentacle holding his arm shriveled and released him. Dom's upper body dropped.

Cazzo. He watched the ground rush up at him. Then the other tentacle released him and he fell. He landed hard on his belly, and he grunted.

He lifted his head. Arden was running toward him.

Her gaze met his, and he couldn't help but smile. Fierce, molten anger was driving his gorgeous woman.

But before he could push to his feet, the ground opened up beneath him.

Fuck.

There were more tentacles directly below him, wriggling in a giant mass. One coiled around his legs and yanked him down into the disturbed soil.

Dirt covered his head. He spat it out, trying to pull

himself upward. He guessed the main body of the alien beast was buried somewhere below him.

"Dom!" Arden screamed.

"Fucking hell." Griff cursed right above Dom's head.

Dom twisted and kicked, trying to stab at the tentacles. They were glowing with a green-blue light, like the glow worms.

Suddenly, a hand reached down and gripped Dom's wrist. He looked into Arden's face.

"I've got you," she cried.

"Get out of here," he growled.

"No! Fight. We're getting you out."

Griff was beside Arden, digging desperately in the dirt to try and get Dom loose.

Dom kicked his legs, but the tentacles kept their tight hold on him. They yanked again, and he sank downward another few inches.

Arden heaved, her face strained.

"Shit, we have more raptors incoming," Tane said in their earpiece. "We're heavily outnumbered."

A sob burst from Arden as she tried to heave Dom upward.

He kept kicking, but the creature wasn't letting him go.

"Berserkers, we need to get out of here!" Tane roared.

Arden kept pulling on Dom. He let his gaze trace over her face. She was so beautiful.

"Go," he said. "Get out."

Shocked violet eyes met his. "No."

"Griff, get her out and go. Keep her safe."

Griff stopped digging, staring at Dom.

"No, damn you," Arden screamed. "I'm *not* losing you, too."

"I want you safe, *bella.* I've always belonged to the dark."

Her face twisted, fierce determination flooding it. "Well, Dominic Santora, I'm dragging you into the light." She tightened her grip on both his wrists and heaved backward. "Now, fight, damn you!"

CHAPTER FOURTEEN

Tears were streaming down Arden's face. Inside, she was on fire.

She'd just found him. She sure as hell *wasn't* losing him.

She gripped Dom's wrists harder. His lower body was buried in the churned up dirt, the tentacles wrapped around him.

No way was she giving up. Dom was hers, and she wasn't letting the Gizzida take him.

Laser fire exploded nearby, and suddenly Griff slammed into her. Her hands slipped off Dom, and Griff's big body pressed her flat, covering her completely.

"Fucking too many of them," Ash yelled.

She heard a guttural growl and looked up. A raptor was almost on top of them, aiming its weapon.

No. Arden couldn't breathe.

"Need some help?"

The gravelly voice echoed in Arden's ear. *Marcus.*

She felt Griff shift above her, and she turned her head.

Hell Squad strode into the fight.

"Hell Squad, you ready to go to hell?" Marcus yelled.

"Hell, yeah," his squad responded. "The devil needs an ass kicking!"

The crack of a sniper rifle echoed loudly in the tunnel, and the raptor standing above Arden jolted. It toppled backward.

"Yeah, baby," Shaw said.

"Nice shot, babe," Claudia drawled.

Laser fire joined the berserkers as Hell Squad launched into the skirmish. Gabe barreled into the fight like a linebacker. Nearby, Reed was firing a modified carbine, firing more cineole. Marcus and Cruz fought side by side. Claudia was providing her man with cover as Shaw fired his rifle.

Suddenly, Selena ran in close to Arden and Griff, landing on her knees beside them.

"Are you okay?" The alien woman's face was streaked with sweat, blood, and dirt.

Arden nodded. "Dom needs help."

Griff slid off her, and they both turned back to the hole. Dom had slid lower and his face was partially covered in dirt. With a cry, Arden lunged for him.

His fingers closed on hers.

"*Bella*." He coughed, spitting away the dirt from his mouth.

"I'm here."

Selena moved closer and thrust her hands into the dirt. A pulse of energy filled the air and Arden gasped.

Suddenly, the tentacles went wild. Dom grunted, pain on his face. Then the tentacles started to shrivel.

"There." Selena dropped back, her face lined with exhaustion.

Griff and Arden both grabbed Dom's arms and heaved backward.

He came free of the ground with a shower of dirt.

Sobbing, Arden threw herself at him. His arms wrapped around her, hugging her tight.

"We've got more raptors," Marcus called out. "We need to go."

Dom pulled Arden to her feet. His balance was off, and she wedged her shoulder under his arm. They closed in with the berserkers. Hell Squad walked backward, all of them firing.

Then Arden's drone beeped.

She glanced at the screen on her wrist. "No, no."

"What is it?" Dom asked.

She looked up, trying to control her panic. "There are more raptors coming in from the tunnel entrance."

"Shit." He swiveled, staring down the entrance to the tunnel. "We're trapped."

Tane cursed.

She watched in horror as the raptors stomped into view. These ones were bigger, their shoulders covered in spikes and their eyes wild. The berserkers had encountered them before, and nicknamed them super raptors. Dread curdled in her gut. They were wilder and more savage than regular raptors.

The super raptors opened fire first, the sharp stench

of poison filling the air. Dom yanked another knife off his belt, and even though he was limping, he threw it.

All around her, the berserkers and Hell Squad threw cineole grenades and fired their carbines.

Selena stood still, her gaze narrowed on the grenades.

She held out a slender hand to Tane. "Give me a grenade."

He glared at her for a beat, then set one in her slender palm. Her fingers closed around it.

"What are you—?"

Selena swiveled and started walking toward the super raptors.

"Selena!" With a curse, Tane followed right behind her.

"Fuck," Hemi bit out. He kept firing his carbine.

With a gentle throw, Selena tossed the grenade into the air. A second later, it popped open, cineole bursting free.

Then Selena closed her eyes and raised her hands.

A gust of wind rushed into the tunnel. It flowed past Arden, rustling her hair. It swirled around Selena and Tane, tearing the tie out of Selena's hair. Her silver-white locks blew back from her face.

The alien woman's skin started to glow. Above on the tunnel roof, the glow worms flared, so bright it hurt to look at them.

Arden threw up a hand and she saw the others shielding their eyes.

Only Tane didn't bother, keeping his gaze locked on Selena.

An arc of light shot out from Selena's palms, like

lightning, and ignited the cineole spray floating in the air. It blazed, flowing out toward all the raptors. It moved around the tunnel, leaving the berserkers and Hell Squad untouched.

Arden stared, her mouth dropping open. Dom's arm tightened around her.

"Fuck me," Hemi muttered.

The raptors started shrieking, dropping their weapons. They clawed at their faces as their skin burned. Blood flowed from their eyes, noses, ears, and mouths.

"Go!" Tane bellowed.

The squad leader wrapped an arm around Selena's waist and lifted her off her feet.

Dom kept his arm tight around Arden as they broke into a jog. They skirted the writhing, screeching super raptors.

Together, with the berserkers and Hell Squad, they ran toward the tunnel entrance.

DOM BARELY REGISTERED the pain in his body as he stepped out of the tunnel.

He was alive. Dappled sunshine fell over him and he sucked in a breath of fresh air.

Beside him, Arden was blinking as her eyes adjusted to the light. Her drone hovered silently above her. Behind them in the darkness, the raptors continued to scream, and the smell of burning flesh wafted out toward them.

He glanced over at Selena. She was standing in the

circle of Tane's arms. The alien woman's skin was still glowing, but she looked tired and shaken.

Griff touched his ear. "Indy?"

"Oh, my fucking God." Indy's half sob came over the line. "Are you okay? Is everyone all right?"

"We're out of the tunnel," Griff said. "A little battered, but everyone's alive."

"Thank God," Indy said. "The bomb?"

"It was a fake," Tane growled. "Let Holmes know we didn't find the bomb."

"Ah, hell. Will do. Get home now."

Ahead, the rugged form of a Z6-Hunter was parked on an angle—Hell Squad's ride. Thankfully, the Gizzida hadn't touched the vehicle, or the berserkers' bikes.

"They probably didn't expect any of us to come out of the tunnel alive," Arden said quietly.

Dom didn't give a shit about his bike. He spun her around to face him.

"Dom."

He yanked her up on her toes and she came eagerly. He cupped her cheek. She was dirty, her hair tangled, and gore splattered her armor.

She was beautiful.

And she was his. His reward. Everything he'd endured in his life was worth it just to hold her.

He lowered his head and kissed her. She threw her arms around his neck and kissed him back.

"Hey, enough of that." Griff slapped Dom on the back.

Dom rested his forehead on Arden's. He was happy to see her smiling.

Ash appeared. "I need to check you out, Dom."

He nodded. Ash's gaze was on Dom's twisted, broken armor. The tentacles had made a mess of it. The medic pulled a piece of chest armor off, then pushed Dom's T-shirt up.

Ash hissed. "Hell, Dom. You've got bad bruising. You could have some internal bleeding."

"I'm fine."

Arden stiffened. "Internal bleeding is not fine."

Dom smoothed a hand over her hair. "I know when I'm hurt bad. I promise you, I'm okay."

Ash nodded. "Get the doc to check you over when we get back to base."

"How about we get the hell out of here?" Marcus suggested.

"Thanks for the help," Tane said.

Marcus nodded. "Our pleasure."

Hell Squad headed for the Hunter. Levi and Hemi were limping and moving cautiously. Dom knew they must be banged up pretty bad, as well.

But they were all still standing.

Dom rolled his bike out onto the track and swung on. Arden settled behind him. She was a slight weight against his back, but she was *everything* to him.

"The drone?" he asked.

"It'll follow."

The Hunter headed off. Around him, the berserkers started their bikes. With a nod, Tane headed out first, Selena sitting quietly behind him, resting against his back.

The rest of the squad followed and Dom pulled into

line. As they bumped down the track, his relief at being alive dissolved.

The aliens had tricked them. There'd been no bomb. It was still out there, somewhere.

As though she could read his thoughts, Arden's arms tightened around him. He dropped a hand, touching where her fingers rested on his abdomen.

It didn't matter. He had a lot to live for now. They'd find the fucking bomb and stop it.

Before, he'd been fighting for redemption.

Now, he was fighting for love.

As they neared the end of the track, two Hawks swept into view overhead. There were also a few smaller, swifter shapes that shot through the air.

Darkswifts. Squad Nine was keeping an eye on the skies.

The track ended at the wide clearing where they'd started. Dom pulled to a stop near the Hunter.

Everyone was battered, but they were alive to fight another day.

"Dom, get your woman into the Hawk," Griff said. "I'll get your bike loaded."

Dom eyed his friend. "I know you're trying to get me to sit down."

Griff smiled. "You did get squeezed by alien tentacles. Figured you needed a rest."

Dom shot his friend the finger.

"Hawk, now," Arden said, voice firm.

"You getting bossy on me, *bella*?"

She kept her arm tight around his back. "If I have to."

Dom waited while Arden deactivated the combat

drone. They had a brief tug of war over the heavy device before she sighed and let him have it. He set it down inside the Hawk. Then he boosted Arden in and tried to hide his grimace as he followed, pain flaring.

"Nice to see you guys alive." Finn appeared in the doorway from the cockpit. "You find the bomb?"

Dom shook his head. "It was a trap."

"Damn." Finn looked at his boots, then lifted his head. "We'll find it."

Dom dropped into a seat and pulled Arden into his lap.

She nuzzled against his chest. "I feel safe right here."

"Always, *bella*. My arms will always be safe for you."

They held each other, and Dom lost the battle against the pain. He drifted a little, breathing in Arden's scent.

It didn't take long to get the bikes loaded. Before he knew it, the rest of his squad was all seated.

"Time to go home," Arden murmured.

The Hawk lifted off. *Yeah, time to go home.*

CHAPTER FIFTEEN

A s the Hawk flew smoothly through the air, Arden stayed curled on Dom's lap. She'd be happy not moving from this position, ever. Still, it would be a relief to get back to the Enclave.

Suddenly, the Hawk veered sharply to the right, banking into a hard turn. She was flung against Dom's chest, and all of the berserkers cursed.

"Finn?" Tane called out.

"Hold on," the Hawk pilot yelled. "We have company."

Everybody swiveled to look out the side windows. Arden watched several ptero ships whizz past the Hawk, and her heart leaped into her throat.

Memories of that night on the street hammered in her head, and she clamped her nails into her palm.

"Mine!" Hemi leaped up, jumping onto the auto-turret mounted on the side of the Hawk.

"Dom..." Her fingers clenched on his arm.

"It'll be okay, *bella*." But there was an intense undertone to his voice.

As Hemi started firing from the autoturret, Tane pushed the side door open, and a rush of wind filled the back of the Hawk. The squad leader lifted his carbine.

All around her, she watched the berserkers tensing, carbines in hand. These men might be rough and crude, but they were heroes to the core, always ready to fight.

As Hemi and Tane fired on the ptero, the Hawk veered again, then pulled upright. Arden clamped her hand onto the seat in front of her. She knew Finn was the best Hawk pilot at the Enclave. He'd get them out of this.

Something struck the quadcopter and it shuddered. Tane swung around and slammed into the side wall.

"There are three of the fuckers," Hemi bit out.

Arden leaned forward, peering through the windows. The pteros were racing through the clouds. She watched as one of the triangular-shaped ships turned and followed the other Hawk.

Then several smaller, dark shapes shot past.

"Yeah," Levi cheered.

She blinked and smiled, realizing it was her squad in the Darkswifts. Her pulse pounded. She prayed for her friends to stay safe, and for Squad Nine to take these pteros down.

"Erickson, you there?"

Mackenna's voice came through the comm in the cockpit.

"I'm here, Mac," Finn answered.

"We have some smaller, flying aliens on our tails. Never seen them before, but they're small, fast, and vicious. Managed to tear a good hole in Sienna and Theron's Darkswift."

"Wonderful. I see them." Finn raised his voice. "We have more unfriendlies incoming. No idea what these things are."

Tane shook his head and looked out the side of the Hawk. Arden watched the man's muscled body tense.

"They're birds of some kind. Covered in gray scales and spikes."

Arden swallowed, and then spotted four of the creatures. They were about the size of a large dog, with leathery, bat-like wings, sharp, black beaks, and a back covered in long, pointy spikes.

Hemi swiveled on the autoturret, and laser fire arced through the sky. "See how you like this."

The laser fire clipped one of the dino birds. The alien let out a squawk, and its leathery wings flared out. It tumbled in a ball and fell downward.

A ptero swung in close and something shot out of the side of it. A bolt of fire hit the autoturret, and it exploded. Hemi was knocked off his seat by the shockwave, his big body flying back into the Hawk.

"Hemi!" Tane yelled.

The berserker groaned from the floor. "I'm okay."

Ash hurried over to help Hemi, while Tane eyed the smoking ruin of the autoturret. With a sharp squawk, one of the Gizzida birds flew in close, beak snapping.

Dom's arms tightened on Arden.

Tane gripped the side of the door and fired his carbine at the creature.

Selena launched to her feet and staggered toward Tane.

"Sit down," he bit out. He didn't look away from the scope of his weapon as he kept firing.

Selena ignored him and balanced right at the edge of the Hawk. Tane's left hand flashed out, clamping around her wrist.

But the alien woman didn't seem to notice. Her gaze was firmly glued outside. Arden glanced out of the door. Suddenly, the clouds nearby began to boil and thicken. Arden gasped. Selena was somehow controlling the clouds.

Tane kept firing.

The cloud cover hid the pteros from view.

"She's giving us cover," Dom said.

Then, without warning, one of the spiked birds flew right into the Hawk. It knocked into Selena, sending her spinning into Tane.

The alien bird landed on the floor of the Hawk. Dom cursed and shoved Arden off the seat, covering her with his body. Around her, the berserkers were shouting and cursing.

She raised her head and came eye to eye with the alien creature.

Above the sharp, black beak were two burning-red eyes. Its spikes bristled around its scaly head. With a sharp squawk, it launched itself forward. Its razor-sharp beak hit the metal floor right near Arden's hand. It left a dent.

"Oh, God." She pushed backward and already felt Dom moving. He gripped her armor, yanking her back.

The bird launched forward again. Arden raised her legs and kicked the creature.

Before it could attack again, a body moved past her. Dom's knives flashed in the light. With no fear, he dodged the sharp beak and spikes, and stabbed at the bird's underbelly.

In that instant, the Hawk turned abruptly, tilting to the left. Arden, Dom, and the Gizzida bird started sliding...right toward the open door of the Hawk.

A scream caught in Arden's throat. Instinct had her scrambling to grab on to something. She watched as the Gizzida bird flew out of the side of the Hawk with an awkward flap of its wings. In the air, it tried desperately to right itself.

Then in horror, she watched Dom slide out right after it.

Tane lunged for him and missed.

"Dom!" Arden slid closer to the edge, horror and pain exploding inside her. Her eyes stayed glued to her man, watching as he plummeted through the air, away from the quadcopter.

"Dom! Dom!" Her voice broke. *No.* She couldn't lose him.

She was about to shoot out of the Hawk herself, when Tane grabbed her with one strong arm. He yanked her back, gripping the edge of the door to keep them in place. He was looking grimly at Dom's falling form.

"No." Arden shook her head. "*No.*" Hysteria welled. "Help him."

"I can't." Tane's words sounded ripped out of him.

She averted her eyes, unwilling to watch Dom fall,

and her gaze snagged on her combat drone still resting on the seat. Her eyes widened. She wouldn't lose the man she loved.

"Drone, activate."

Lights blinked on.

"Retrieve!" she yelled. "Retrieve Dominic Santora."

The combat drone lifted, then shot out of the Hawk, almost brushing her hair as it moved.

She saw it in the clouds, then it swiveled and plunged downward through the sky.

Dom. Please. Please. The words became a prayer, echoing in her head.

Arden didn't look away. She knew this was a long shot. The combat drone wasn't designed to carry the weight of a full-grown man in armor.

She gripped Tane's arm. She'd lost sight of Dom, but she kept staring at the open air below.

Dom. Please. Please.

The Hawk leveled out and there was a silence in the back of the aircraft.

"Guys, what's going on?" Indy asked.

Arden's throat closed. She couldn't speak.

"Dom fell out of the Hawk." Tane's voice was harsh.

"No," Indy whispered.

Arden stared at the clouds below, waiting, waiting.

"Arden, come away from the door," Tane said quietly.

No. Dom. Please. Please. A tear tracked down her cheek. She couldn't handle the loss. She couldn't handle having her heart ripped out of her chest again. Not when she'd only just put it back together with Dom's help.

"I can't lose him." She met Tane's deep-brown eyes, full of his own shadows. "I won't survive it again."

He pulled her closer. "Whatever life throws at you, however hard it grinds you down in the dirt, you keep getting back up. That's all we can do."

She shook her head, a sob breaking out of her.

She looked back at the empty sky. *Dom.*

Suddenly, something shot up out of the clouds. She gasped, and heard Tane suck in a sharp breath.

Like it was drunk, the combat drone wobbled, heading back toward the Hawk. Below it, Dom dangled, hanging on, his face strained. The drone flew in through the side of the Hawk and Dom let go. His body crashed into Arden, and they slid across the floor.

She clamped her arms and legs around him. "Dom, oh, my God."

"Fuck," Griff bit out.

"I never want to do that again," Dom said quietly.

Arden couldn't hold back her sobs. She held onto him tighter.

"I'm okay, *bella*. I'm okay."

Tane slammed the door of the Hawk shut. His chin dropped to his chest. "Hell."

Then Griff was there. He grabbed Dom in a hard hug.

Arden refused to let him go, holding onto him tightly. His heart beat firmly in his chest, and she clung to the sound. Her sobs morphed to silent tears.

Tane dropped heavily into a seat. He shoved the combat drone onto the seat beside him. "Finn, how we doing?"

"The Darkswifts shot the pteros out of the sky," the pilot reported. "Alien birds disappeared. Squad Nine is headed back to base with the other Hawk."

"Thank fuck," Hemi muttered.

"Dom okay?" Finn asked.

Tane glanced at Dom. "Doubt he's planning to take flying lessons any time soon."

Arden felt Dom's fingers flex on her. Hysterical laughter welled in her chest. Trust the berserkers to make a joke about a life and death situation.

"Get us home, Finn," Tane said.

Dom scooped Arden into his arms and she buried her face against his neck. He sat with her in his lap.

"Thanks for rescuing me, *bella*."

A half laugh, half sob ripped out of her. Something in his tone said he wasn't just talking about saving him from the fall.

Then he sank a hand in her hair and tipped her head back. She stared at those dark eyes, that handsome face. *Hers*.

"I love you, Dom."

Something flared in his eyes—a volatile mix of emotion.

"Before, I had a safe, easy, predictable life. I loved it. I loved my husband and our children. Now that life is gone. I'll always remember it, cherish it. But life moves on. The sun still rises, babies are born, people die." She cupped his stubbled cheek. "I want to wake up with you every day. I want to make a life with you that's anything but safe or predictable."

He dropped his mouth to hers and kissed her.

And he kept kissing her. Long, drugging kisses.

Both of them were heedless of the laughter and wolf whistles around them. There was only the two of them, and they took their time.

When Dom did lift his mouth from hers, Arden felt more than a little lightheaded. She saw Griff was grinning widely at them. Nearby, Selena had a small smile on her face that looked almost wistful.

"I don't know much about love, *bella*," Dom said. "But the way I feel about you overwhelms me. I know I'm yours. And together, you can teach me about love."

"Tell me," she said.

"I love you."

"In Italian."

"*Ti amo.*"

She pressed her nose to his, cupping the side of his head.

He lowered his voice. "I'll whisper other things in Italian to you later."

With another hiccupping laugh, she wrapped her arms around him and held on tight.

Before she knew it, they were landing back at the Enclave.

When Tane opened the side door, the general was standing there, waiting with Squad Nine. Arden's squad all looked sweaty and tired, their damp hair stuck to their heads.

When Roth caught her eyes, the man's gaze swept over her. He eyed Dom suspiciously, but when Arden smiled, Roth relaxed and nodded.

As soon as Hemi climbed out of the Hawk, Cam

appeared. She threw her arms around her man and he bent her over, kissing her noisily.

Hell Squad moved over to join the group, having landed just before them.

"The bomb was a fake," the general said.

Tane nodded. "Gizzida planted a nice little trap for us."

A muscle ticked in Holmes' jaw. He pressed one hand to his hip. "We rest. We regroup. Then we find the damn thing."

All around, the soldiers nodded.

"We do what we do best," Arden said.

Everyone turned around to look at her.

"We persist. We keep trying. We never give up." She leaned into Dom. "We all have too much to live for."

Nate

NATE CALDWELL MADE his way silently through the trees, his axe resting on his shoulder. As he neared the clearing ahead, he heard a sound overhead and froze.

A quadcopter shot by, an alien ship following closely behind. Laser fire arrowed through the air, and then he lost sight of them.

Quietly, he stayed in the shadow of the trees, waiting to see if he could glimpse or hear anything else. He'd heard the commotion to the north earlier. The humans had fought another skirmish with the aliens.

He hoped the soldiers had given the scaly bastards hell.

He stared into the sky where he'd seen the aircraft. A part of him, the warrior, wanted to grab his weapons and join the fight.

Fight. Kill. Protect.

Gritting his teeth, Nate tamped the battle urge back down. Thinking of soldiers made him think of his old team. For a second, the Blue Mountains disappeared, and instead there was hot desert sun, the sound of laser fire, the shouts of his fellow Marines.

Then there was pain and the rich scent of blood.

His fingers dug into the handle of his axe. He dragged in a deep breath. Then another. And another.

For the next few minutes, Nate worked through his breathing routine until his pulse rate slowed.

The breathing techniques were the only thing he'd taken from the short time he'd spent with a therapist after he'd left the Coalition Marines. That had been long ago. After a different, long-gone war.

That battle was long gone, like his fellow Marines.

Nate let out a sharp whistle and his dog bounded out of the trees. The blue heeler was lean and fit. He rubbed the dog's head. "Come on, Blue. No more fighting for us."

After several deployments in the Middle East, Nate had come back from war to his family home in Colorado. He'd had trouble adjusting and settling back into regular life. PTSD, they'd told him. There had been medication, group therapy, prolonged exposure therapy.

He shifted the axe, and crouched down to pick up the

pile of wood he'd chopped earlier. He tucked the wood under his arm.

Nothing had helped him back then. He'd had horrific nightmares, angry outbursts at his worried family, then he'd started drinking. After that, he'd started fighting.

He blew out a breath

Nate had been drowning, and when he'd broken a man's jaw and another man's arm in a bar fight, he knew he was spiraling down and nothing could stop it.

Then he'd learned that he'd inherited a cabin in the Australian Blue Mountains, from a great-aunt. Old aunt Janine had been a battle-axe. The few times he'd seen her as a kid, she'd scowled at him and told him not to bring his dirty shoes inside her house.

He had no idea why she'd left the cabin to him, but she'd saved his life.

Through the trees, his cabin came into view. It was small, made from wood, with a tiny deck at the back. It hadn't changed much from when Janine had lived here. He'd repaired parts of it, including most of the roof. He enjoyed working with his hands.

Pausing, Nate breathed deep, pulling in the crisp mountain air.

He'd come here just a few months before the alien invasion and gone off-grid. He'd disappeared from the regular world, keeping in touch with his family via email. He'd left all the responsibility and expectations of life behind. The cabin had a generator, water from a stream, well-used garden beds. It was completely self-contained.

Then the aliens had come and destroyed the world.

After the invasion, he'd followed the news on the radio until the stations had gone silent.

He'd tried to contact his family, but there'd been nothing.

Shit. He blindly scanned the trees and hoped his parents and brother and sister had survived. He wished he'd talked to them more. Wished he hadn't caused them so much worry and heartache.

Nate had seen plenty of the aliens in the mountains. Luckily, the bastards didn't like the trees. He'd done recon, gathering intel on them, but steering clear of their big ugly, scaled asses.

He dumped the wood by his back door.

He also knew about Blue Mountain Base, and the survivors who'd gathered there. He'd watched them, too. Knew about the squads.

He'd seen them fighting back. He'd watched the Hawks in the sky, seen the armor-clad soldiers. A part of him had yearned to help.

With a huge swing, he thrust the axe into the wood pile. Then he reached up and yanked his damp T-shirt over his head. He rubbed his sweaty face with it.

Nate barely had any body fat. Living off the land and what he hunted, as well as being active every day, kept him in better shape than his Marine days.

Sometimes he missed a beer with friends. Conversation. Sometimes he missed women—their soft bodies, sweet smells, and sliding his hard cock into warmth instead of his callused hand.

Shaking his head, he stomped up the steps and into his cabin.

Blue Mountain Base had been destroyed by the aliens months ago. The survivors had left in a convoy, and he assumed they'd found another shelter. He still saw Hawks in the sky on occasion, so he knew they hadn't died.

The battle-hardened Marine in him rose up again. *You could be helping, using your skills to fight.*

No. He stomped over to the old-fashioned kitchen, pulled out one of Aunt Janine's heavy, etched glasses, and filled it with water. He drank it in two large gulps.

He'd done all the fighting he could. He was thirty-seven years old and still had nightmares. Even if he'd wanted to, he couldn't face fighting the aliens on top of that.

Wrenching open a cupboard, he grabbed Blue's bowl. He had to feed his damn dog. The blue heeler was sitting beside him, waiting patiently. He watched Nate with soulful, gold eyes.

"Just you and me, Blue."

Blue's tail thumped the faded, lino floor.

With a grunt, Nate dumped some meat from a rabbit he'd caught that morning onto the bowl and set it on the floor. Blue dove in.

Being alone kept Nate sane. He straightened, looking out of the window at the trees beyond. And alone was how he was going to stay.

CHAPTER SIXTEEN

Dom rubbed the towel over his damp hair, then tossed it on the floor. He reached for his clothes, and put on his trousers and a black, button-down shirt.

As he did up the buttons, he looked at the bathroom door. Arden was still soaking in the tub.

She'd earned it.

She'd held her own out there. Dom smiled. His woman had been *magnificent*.

After they'd returned to base, Emerson had checked them over. Apart from a few bruises, they'd been given the all clear.

He headed back to the bathroom, and when he stepped into the doorway, his chest tightened.

Arden had just gotten out of the tub, and stood on the mat, naked and beautiful. He let his gaze roam over her. All that smooth, white skin, the wet, tangled hair at her shoulders. She had a slender, elegant body that hid so much strength.

Desire stormed through him, followed by need, and a deeper, intense emotion he now knew was love.

This woman *loved* him. She was the first person to ever say the words to him.

And the only woman who would ever hear the words from his lips.

She must have sensed him, because she turned and smiled.

"I can't believe that you love me," he blurted out.

Her face softened. "I'll spend every day showing you I do until you never doubt it."

Dom couldn't breathe. His need rose up, wrapping around his throat and clutching at his heart. He strode to her, sweeping an arm around her.

He lowered his head. "I love you so much."

Her fingers slid into his hair. "You deserve to be loved, Dom."

He took her mouth with his, thrusting his tongue inside. The need inside him was greedy, starving for her.

It turned off all rational thought. *Mine, mine, mine.* He pulled her down onto the mat, covering her with his body. He knew he was being rough, was out-of-control, but he couldn't seem to stop. His body was trembling. He needed to be surrounded by her, soaked in her scent.

He tore his trousers open, freeing his cock. He shoved her legs apart.

Then he thrust hard.

Arden arched into him, screaming.

"Arden." *Cazzo*, he'd hurt her.

But then she cupped his face, her legs locking around his hips. "Shh. Take what you need. I want you."

He slid a hand between their bodies, rubbing her clit. He felt the wetness of her around his hard cock. His Arden wanted him with the same ferocity he wanted her.

Dom pulled back and plunged inside her.

"Yes," she hissed.

He kept up the pounding rhythm, his thrusts mindless. And she took it, all of it, and asked for more.

As they coupled on the floor like animals in heat, all Dom could feel, see, smell was Arden. His woman.

"I love you." She sang the words. "I love you. Light and dark, good and bad, my feelings for you will never change."

"*Bella.*" She tore him open. She put him back together.

And then she was coming, throwing her head back. Her gorgeous, elegant face was flushed, and small, husky noises came from her throat.

The pleasure was almost painful. His muscles strained as he kept thrusting inside her.

Everything inside him contracted, then exploded outwards. He lodged deep inside her and roared as he came.

ARDEN STOOD BESIDE INDY, both of them standing at attention behind General Holmes.

He was talking with the leader of the Groom Lake Base in the USA.

The middle-aged, African-American woman styled her hair in a neat and tidy bob and wore a black, military uniform. She had a serious look on her face as she listened to Holmes.

At her back, stood a silent man in fatigues. He'd been introduced as her head of security.

Arden had snuck a glance at him more than a few times. It was hard not to. He was tall and well-built, with bulging biceps. His strong jaw was covered in not-quite-a-beard, but definitely more than scruff.

And he had flat, impenetrable gray eyes.

He was the kind of man who you'd want on your side of the battle.

"I'm disappointed to hear that the bomb wasn't destroyed, Adam," Major General Michaela Marshall said. "I'm sure it must be disappointing for you, and your squads as well."

Holmes nodded. "We aren't giving up. We're working hard to find it."

The major general nodded. "And my head of security —" she looked at the man beside her "—Captain Dak Vaughn is heading up our search here at Groom Lake."

"We have nothing to report yet," Dak Vaughn said.

Oh. The man had a smooth, sexy baritone that was completely at odds with his tough, military appearance.

Indy made a small sound. When Arden glanced her way, her friend rolled her eyes back in her head.

Holmes nodded. "We'll keep in communication about the search, and with the other bases. We'll keep you updated."

"Good hunting, Adam," the Groom Lake leader said.

As the screen blinked off, Holmes rose. "We need to get to the Garden for the update meeting."

Arden nodded. The general had called a gathering of all the Enclave residents to update them on the situation.

Everyone was well aware their survival hung in the balance.

Arden and Indy followed Holmes out of the Command Center.

"Did you hear that man's voice?" Indy made a humming sound.

"You have a man," Arden reminded her.

"And I've loved Griff practically all my life, but Dak Vaughn's voice...it's like being dipped naked in melted chocolate and then having it licked off you."

Arden giggled.

Indy glanced at her and smiled. "That's the sweetest sound, Ard. I'm so glad that your hunky Italian is making you happy."

In front of them, Holmes made a choked sound. "You know I can hear you."

Arden bit her lip and Indy's smile simply widened.

"Yep," Indy replied unrepentantly. "You might be the boss man, but I'm pretty sure you know exactly how Liberty ended up with your baby in her belly."

Holmes just held up a hand and kept walking.

Arden and Indy shared another glance, then burst into laughter.

When they finally reached the Garden, they found the space crowded. Sunshine filtered in from the open roof, and the grass was lush and green. Remembering sleeping on that grass in the arms of her very own dark knight, Arden scanned the crowd.

She saw Levi and Chrissy tossing a ball with a young

boy. Arden knew Chrissy had helped rescue the boy from Gizzida captivity. The trio were smiling.

Nearby, several kids had made the bad decision to throw mud at each other. One boy scooped it out of a garden bed and tossed it at his friends. Arden shook her head, imagining that her Emmett would be right in there for an impromptu mud fight. Another boy scooped up a handful of mud and tossed it. But his aim was way off.

It hit the back of Marcus Steele's T-shirt.

As the squad leader slowly turned, the boys froze in horror. Beside Marcus, Elle was trying to hide her smile behind her hand. Marcus' gaze zeroed in on the perpetrators. Then, in a fast move for a man his size, Marcus scooped up some mud and swung his arm.

The mud splattered the boy's shirt. His eyes went wide, then he saw the smile on Marcus' face. The boy started laughing and his friends joined in.

Light in the darkness. Arden watched the mud fight escalate. That's what kept all the survivors going. Even when the shadows surrounded them, they found the glimmer of light that kept them going. Her lips curved. Or they found their own dark knight to guide them through the darkness.

Shaw and Claudia had joined in the fun, although, it looked like the lovers were more interested in getting each other than the kids. Arden watched Claudia shove a handful of mud down the back of her man's shirt with a gleeful laugh.

Shaw arched his back and grabbed Claudia's long ponytail. "You'll pay for that, Frost."

Shaking her head, Arden turned. She spotted Alyssa

from Mount Wilson and her smile faded. The woman stood a little apart from the people around her, her face blank, her eyes downcast. Grief covered her like a cloud. She couldn't see the light yet.

Arden pressed her lips together. The woman would need time, and Arden prayed that sooner, rather than later, she would find some peace. In her heart, she sent up a small message. *Jason, Beth, and Emmett, if you spot two kids up there, Annie and Mickey, give them a hug from their mama.*

Next, Arden spotted her squad. Taylor, Cam, and Sienna waved at her and she waved back. Beside Squad Nine stood the berserkers, all looking rough and sexy.

Arden's gaze fell on Dom as he stood talking with Griff. Her chest swelled with warmth. Looking at him was a reminder that she was very much alive. She started in his direction.

Suddenly, something brushed her ankle, almost tripping her over. She looked down and saw a crawling baby grinning at her, showing off a small collection of tiny teeth.

"Hey, there."

The baby gurgled.

"Sorry. She's quick." Cruz appeared, scooping his baby up with one muscled, tattooed arm. He kissed the little girl's neck, making her giggle. "Escape artist in the making." With a smile, he turned, tucked baby Kari into the curve of his arm, and headed toward his woman, Santha.

"There go my ovaries," Indy muttered. "I want to see Griff cuddling our baby now."

Arden watched Cruz. "I don't think I want any more kids."

Indy reached out and grabbed her hand.

Arden smiled, bittersweet pain piercing her heart. "I raised my kids." She'd have to talk about it with Dom, but until the Gizzida bombs were destroyed, there was no way she could bring a child into this world.

"You deserve whatever you want," Indy said.

"For the moment, I just want to have hot sex with my hunky Italian."

Indy broke out in wild laughter.

"What's this about hunky Italians?" Griff appeared, a mock scowl on his face.

A hard arm circled Arden's waist and Dom pressed a kiss to her temple. She leaned into him, breathing in his cologne. She spun, sliding her arms around his lean waist.

"Hi," she said.

"Hi." His face was as dark and intense as always.

Holmes stepped up on the bench of one of the picnic tables in the front of the crowd, his woman Liberty standing nearby. He cleared his throat.

Everyone quieted.

"By now, you'll all have heard that our squads walked into a trap in the Blue Mountains."

You could have heard a pin drop.

"The bomb wasn't there."

Now, there were a few unhappy murmurs.

"But despite a vicious fight, our people made it back safely. We're continuing the search for the bomb, as well as staying in regular contact with all the other survivor bases. All of us have our squads out there, searching." Holmes paused, his blue gaze scanning the crowd. "*Nothing* will stop us, deter us, or frighten us. We *will* find all three bombs, and we will neutralize them."

A man raised his voice and called out, "The Gizzida won't stop either. They'll keep trying to destroy us."

Holmes nodded. "And we'll keep refusing to let them."

Now, there were a few laughs.

"The road ahead isn't going to be easy," the general said. "When has it been? Some of us might die in sacrifice to the fight. But all of us will fight, in our own ways, from the cooks who feed us, to the soldiers who protect us."

He glanced over to where Liberty stood, her golden locks shining in the sun and her hand resting on her pregnant belly. She looked at him and smiled—a warm, sexy, love-filled smile.

A smile flickered on Holmes' lips as he turned back to the crowd.

"We fight," he said. "For love, for hope, for our home. Every day, we fight so the aliens won't win. They *can't* have our home."

Cheers erupted.

"They *can't* have our people." Holmes raised his voice.

The cheers got louder.

"And they can't have our planet!"

The whole crowd erupted, cheering and slapping backs.

"He makes it sound easy," Arden murmured.

Dom pulled her tighter against him. "It's not easy, but

we take it one day at a time. And we hold on to hope." He dropped a kiss to her lips. "Feel like sketching?"

She lifted her shoulder. "Maybe."

"I'll be a willing model."

She smiled, letting her gaze wander down his chest. "My nude model?"

"Any way you want me, Arden. I'm all yours. Whatever you need from me, I'll give it to you."

She pressed her palms against his shirt. His heart beat, strong and steady, beneath her palm. And now she knew it beat for her.

"Your heart, my dark knight. That's all I need."

I hope you enjoyed Arden and Dom's story!

Hell Squad will continue with *Hell Squad Survivors*, a novella collection containing stories of survivors outside the Enclave including former Marine Nate Caldwell, Groom Lake Head of Security Captain Dak Vaughn, and Alexander Erickson.

After *Hell Squad Survivors* will be *Tane*, the final action-packed book in the Hell Squad series.
Both coming in 2020.

For more action-packed romance, read on for a preview of the first Eon Warriors adventure, *Edge of Eon*.

Don't miss out! For updates about new releases, action romance info, free books, and other fun stuff, sign up for my VIP mailing list and get your *free box set* containing three action-packed romances.

Visit here to get started: www.annahackettbooks.com

PREVIEW: EDGE OF EON

She shifted on the chair, causing the chains binding her hands to clank together. Eve Traynor snorted. The wrist and ankle restraints were overkill. She was on a low-orbit prison circling Earth. Where the fuck did they think she was going to go?

Eve shifted her shoulders to try to ease the tension from having her hands tied behind her back. For the millionth time, she studied her surroundings. The medium-sized room was empty, except for her chair. Everything from the floor to the ceiling was dull-gray metal. All of the Citadel Prison was drab and sparse. She'd learned every boring inch of it the last few months.

One wide window provided the only break in the otherwise uniform space. Outside, she caught a tantalizing glimpse of the blue-green orb of Earth below.

Her gut clenched and she drank in the sight of her home. Five months she'd been locked away in this prison. Five months since her life had imploded.

She automatically thought of her sisters. She sucked in a deep breath. She hated everything they'd had to go through because of what had happened. Hell, she thought of her mom as well, even though their last contact had been the day after Eve had been imprisoned. Her mom had left Eve a drunken, scathing message.

The door to the room opened, and Eve lifted her chin and braced.

When she saw the dark-blue Space Corps uniform, she stiffened. When she saw the row of stars on the lapel, she gritted her teeth.

Admiral Linda Barber stepped into the room, accompanied by a female prison guard. The admiral's hair was its usual sleek bob of highlighted, ash-blonde hair. Her brown eyes were steady.

Eve looked at the guard. "Take me back to my cell."

The admiral lifted a hand. "Please leave us."

The guard hesitated. "That's against protocol, ma'am—"

"It'll be fine." The admiral's stern voice said she was giving an order, not making a request.

The guard hesitated again, then ducked through the door. It clicked closed behind her.

Eve sniffed. "Say what you have to say and leave."

Admiral Barber sighed, taking a few steps closer. "I know you're angry. You have a right to be—"

"You think?" Eve sucked back the rush of molten anger. "I got tossed under the fucking starship to save a mama's boy. A mama's boy who had no right to be in command of one of Space Corps' vessels."

Shit. Eve wanted to pummel something. Preferably the face of Robert J. Hathaway—golden son of Rear-Admiral Elisabeth Hathaway. A man who, because of family connections, was given captaincy of the *Orion*, even though he lacked the intelligence and experience needed to lead it.

Meanwhile, Eve—a Space Corps veteran—had worked her ass off during her career in the Corps, and had been promised her own ship, only to be denied her chance. Instead, she'd been assigned as Hathaway's second-in-command. To be a glorified babysitter, and to actually run the ship, just without the title and the pay raise.

She'd swallowed it. Swallowed Hathaway's incompetence and blowhard bullshit. Until he'd fucked up. Big-time.

"The Haumea Incident was regrettable," Barber said.

Eve snorted. "Mostly for the people who died. And

definitely for me, since I'm the one shackled to a chair in the Citadel. Meanwhile, I assume Bobby Hathaway is still a dedicated Space Corps employee."

"He's no longer a captain of a ship. And he never will be again."

"Right. Mommy got him a cushy desk job back at Space Corps Headquarters."

The silence was deafening and it made Eve want to kick something.

"I'm sorry, Eve. We all know what happened wasn't right."

Eve jerked on her chains and they clanked against the chair. "And you let it happen. All of Space Corps leadership did, to appease Mommy Hathaway. I dedicated my life to the Corps, and you all screwed me over for an admiral's incompetent son. I got sentenced to prison for *his* mistakes." Stomach turning in vicious circles, Eve looked at the floor, sucking in air. She stared at the soft booties on her feet. Damned inmate footwear. She wasn't even allowed proper fucking shoes.

Admiral Barber moved to her side. "I'm here to offer you a chance at freedom."

Gaze narrowing, Eve looked up. Barber looked... nervous. Eve had never seen the self-assured woman nervous before.

"There's a mission. If you complete it, you'll be released from prison."

Interesting. "And reinstated? With a full pardon?"

Barber's lips pursed and her face looked pinched. "We can negotiate."

So, no. "Screw your offer." Eve would prefer to rot in her cell, rather than help the Space Corps.

The admiral moved in front of her, her low-heeled pumps echoing on the floor. "Eve, the fate of the world depends on this mission."

Barber's serious tone sent a shiver skating down Eve's spine. She met the woman's brown eyes.

"The Kantos are gathering their forces just beyond the boundary at Station Omega V."

Fuck. The Kantos. The insectoid alien race had been nipping at Earth for years. Their humanoid-insectoid soldiers were the brains of the operation, but they encompassed all manner of ugly, insect-like beasts as well.

With the invention of zero-point drives several decades ago, Earth's abilities for space exploration had exploded. Then, thirty years ago, they'd made first contact with an alien species—the Eon.

The Eon shared a common ancestor with the humans of Earth. They were bigger and broader, with a few differing organs, but generally human-looking. They had larger lungs, a stronger, bigger heart, and a more efficiently-designed digestion system. This gave them increased strength and stamina, which in turn made them excellent warriors. Unfortunately, they also wanted nothing to do with Earth and its inferior Terrans.

The Eon, and their fearsome warriors and warships, stayed inside their own space and had banned Terrans from crossing their boundaries.

Then, twenty years ago, the first unfortunate and bloody meeting with the Kantos had occurred.

Since then, the Kantos had returned repeatedly to

nip at the Terran borders—attacking ships, space stations, and colonies.

But it had become obvious in the last year or so that the Kantos had something bigger planned. The Haumea Incident had made that crystal clear.

The Kantos wanted Earth. There were to be no treaties, alliances, or negotiations. They wanted to descend like locusts and decimate everything—all the planet's resources, and most of all, the humans.

Yes, the Kantos wanted to freaking use humans as a food source. Eve suppressed a shudder.

"And?" she said.

"We have to do whatever it takes to save our planet."

Eve tilted her head. "The Eon."

Admiral Barber smiled. "You were always sharp, Eve. Yes, the Eon are the only ones with the numbers, the technology, and the capability to help us repel the Kantos."

"Except they want nothing to do with us." No one had seen or spoken with an Eon for three decades.

"Desperate times call for desperate measures."

Okay, Eve felt that shiver again. She felt like she was standing on the edge of a platform, about to be shoved under the starship again.

"What's the mission?" she asked carefully.

"We want you to abduct War Commander Davion Thann-Eon."

Holy fuck. Eve's chest clenched so tight she couldn't even draw a breath. Then the air rushed into her lungs, and she threw her head back and laughed. Tears ran down her face.

"You're kidding."

But the admiral wasn't laughing.

Eve shook her head. "That's a fucking suicide mission. You want me to abduct the deadliest, most decorated Eon war commander who controls the largest, most destructive Eon warship in their fleet?"

"Yes."

"No."

"Eve, you have a record of making...risky decisions."

Eve shook her head. "I always calculate the risks."

"Yes, but you use a higher margin of error than the rest of us."

"I've always completed my missions successfully." The Haumea Incident excluded, since that was Bobby's brilliant screw-up.

"Yes. That's why we know if anyone has a chance of making this mission a success, it's you."

"I may as well take out a blaster and shoot myself right now. One, I'll never make it into Eon space, let alone aboard the *Desteron*."

Since the initial encounter, they'd collected whatever intel they could on the Eon. Eve had seen secret schematics of that warship. And she had to admit, the thought of being aboard that ship left her a little damp between her thighs. She loved space and flying, and the big, sleek warship was something straight out of her fantasies.

"We have an experimental, top-of-the-line stealth ship for you to use," the admiral said.

Eve carried on like the woman hadn't spoken. "And two, even if I got close to the war commander, he's bigger and stronger than me, not to mention bonded to a fucking deadly alien symbiont that gives him added strength and the ability to create organic armor and weapons with a single thought. I'd be dead in seconds."

"We recovered a...substance that is able to contain the symbiont the Eon use."

Eve narrowed her eyes. "Recovered from where?"

Admiral Barber cleared her throat. "From the wreck of a Kantos ship. It was clearly tech they were developing to use against the Eon."

Shit. "So I'm to abduct the war commander, and then further enrage him by neutralizing his symbiont."

"We believe the containment is temporary, and there is an antidote."

Eve shook her head. "This is beyond insane."

"For the fate of humanity, we have to try."

"*Talk* to them," Eve said. "Use some diplomacy."

"We tried. They refused all contact."

Because humans were simply ants to the Eon. Small, insignificant, an annoyance.

Although, truth be told, humanity only had itself to blame. By all accounts, Terrans hadn't behaved very well at first contact. The meetings with the Eon had turned into blustering threats, different countries trying to make alliances with the aliens while happily stabbing each other in the back.

Now Earth wanted to abduct an Eon war commander. No, not a war commander, *the* war commander. So dumb. She wished she had a hand free so she could slap it over her eyes.

"Find another sacrificial lamb."

The admiral was silent for a long moment. "If you won't do it for yourself or for humanity, then do it for your sisters."

Eve's blood chilled and she cocked her head. "What's this got to do with my sisters?"

"They've made a lot of noise about your imprisonment. Agitating for your freedom."

Eve breathed through her nose. God, she loved her sisters. Still, she didn't know whether to be pleased or pissed. "And?"

"Your sister has shared some classified information with the press about the Haumea Incident."

Eve fought back a laugh. Lara wasn't shy about sharing her thoughts about this entire screwed-up situation. Eve's older sister was a badass Space Corps special forces marine. Lara wouldn't hesitate to take down anyone who pissed her off, the Space Corps included.

"And she had access to information she should not have had access to, meaning your other sister has done some...creative hacking."

Dammit. The rush of love was mixed with some annoyance. Sweet, geeky Wren had a giant, super-smart brain. She was a computer-systems engineer for some company with cutting-edge technology in Japan. It helped keep her baby sister's big brain busy, because Wren hadn't found a computer she couldn't hack.

"Plenty of people are unhappy with what your sisters have been stirring up," Barber continued.

Eve stiffened. She didn't like where this was going.

"I've tried to run interference—"

"Admiral—"

Barber held up a hand. "I can't keep protecting them, Eve. I've been trying, but some of this is even above my pay grade. If you don't do this mission, powers outside of my control will go after them. They'll both end up in a cell right alongside yours until the Kantos arrive and blow this prison out of the sky."

Her jaw tight, Eve's brain turned all the information over. *Fucking fuck.*

"Eve, if there is anyone who has a chance of succeeding on this mission, it's you."

Eve stayed silent.

Barber stepped closer. "I don't care if you do it for yourself, the billions of people of Earth, or your sisters—"

"I'll do it." The words shot out of Eve, harsh and angry.

She'd do it—abduct the scariest alien war commander in the galaxy—for all the reasons the admiral listed—to clear her name, for her freedom, to save the world, and for the sisters she loved.

Honestly, it didn't matter anyway, because the odds of her succeeding and coming back alive were zero.

EVE LEFT THE STARSHIP GYM, towel around her neck, and her muscles warm and limber from her workout.

God, it was nice to work out when it suited her. On the Citadel Prison, exercise time was strictly scheduled, monitored, and timed.

Two crew members came into view, heading down

the hall toward her. As soon as the uniformed men spotted her, they looked at the floor and passed her quickly.

Eve rolled her eyes. Well, she wasn't aboard the *Polaris* to make friends, and she had to admit, she had a pretty notorious reputation. She'd never been one to blindly follow the rules, plus there was the Haumea Incident and her imprisonment. And her family were infamous in the Space Corps. Her father had been a space marine, killed in action in one of the early Kantos encounters. Her mom had been a decorated Space Corps member, but after Eve's dad had died, her mom had started drinking. It had deteriorated until she'd gone off the rails. She'd done it quite publicly, blaming the Space Corps for her husband's death. In the process, she'd forgotten she had three young, grieving girls.

Yep, Eve was well aware that the people you cared for most either left you, or let you down. The employer you worked your ass off for treated you like shit. The only two people in the galaxy that didn't apply to were her sisters.

Eve pushed thoughts of her parents away. Instead, she scanned the starship. The *Polaris* was a good ship. A mid-size cruiser, she was designed for exploration, but well-armed as well. Eve guessed they'd be heading out beyond Neptune about now.

The plan was for the *Polaris* to take her to the edge of Eon space, where she'd take a tiny, two-person stealth ship, sneak up to the *Desteron*, then steal onboard.

Piece of cake. She rolled her eyes.

Back in her small cabin, she took a quick shower,

dressed, and then headed to the ops room. It was a small room close to the bridge that the ship's captain had made available to her.

She stepped inside, and all the screens flickered to life. A light table stood in the center of the room, and everything was filled with every scrap of intel that the Space Corps had on the Eon Empire, their warriors, the *Desteron*, and War Commander Thann-Eon.

It was more than she'd guessed. A lot of it had been classified. There was fascinating intel on the four Eon homeworld planets—Eon, Jad, Felis, and Ath. Each Eon warrior carried their homeworld in their name, along with their clan names. The war commander hailed from the planet Eon, and Thann was a clan known as a warrior clan.

Eve swiped her fingers across the light table and studied pictures of the *Desteron*. They were a few years old and taken from a great distance, but that didn't hide the warship's power.

It was fearsome. Black, sleek, and impressive. It was built for speed and stealth, but also power. It had to be packed with weapons beyond their imagination.

She touched the screen again and slid the image to the side. Another image appeared—the only known picture of War Commander Thann-Eon.

Jesus. The man packed a punch. All Eon warriors looked alike—big, broad-shouldered, muscular. They all had longish hair—not quite reaching the shoulders, but not cut short, either. Their hair usually ranged from dark brown to a tawny, golden-brown. There was no black or blond hair among the Eon. Their skin color ranged from dark-brown to light-brown, as well.

Before first contact had gone sour, both sides had done some DNA testing, and confirmed the Eon and Terrans shared an ancestor.

The war commander was wearing a pitch-black, sleeveless uniform. He was tall, built, with long legs and powerful thighs. He was exactly the kind of man you expected to stride onto a battlefield, pull a sword, and slaughter everyone. He had a strong face, one that shouted power. Eve stroked a finger over the image. He had a square jaw, a straight, almost aggressive nose, and a well-formed brow. His eyes were as dark as space, but shot through with intriguing threads of blue.

"It's you and me, War Commander." If he didn't kill her, first.

Suddenly, sirens blared.

Eve didn't stop to think. She slammed out of the ops room and sprinted onto the bridge.

Inside, the large room was a flurry of activity.

Captain Chen stood in the center of the space, barking orders at his crew.

Her heart contracted. God, she'd missed this so much. The vibration of the ship beneath her feet, her team around her, even the scent of recycled starship air.

"You shouldn't be in here," a sharp voice snapped.

Eve turned, locking gazes with the stocky, bearded XO. Sub-Captain Porter wasn't a fan of hers.

"Leave her," Captain Chen told his second-in-command. "She's seen more Kantos ships than all of us combined."

The captain looked back at his team. "Shields up."

Eve studied the screen and the Kantos ship approaching.

It looked like a bug. It had large, outstretched legs, and a bulky, segmented, central fuselage. It wasn't the biggest ship she'd seen, but it wasn't small, either. It was probably out on some intel mission.

"Sir," a female voice called out. "We're getting a distress call from the *Panama*, a cargo ship en route to Nightingale Space Station. They're under attack from a swarm of small Kantos ships."

Eve sucked in a breath, her hand curling into a fist. This was a usual Kantos tactic. They would overwhelm a ship with their small swarm ships. It had ugly memories of the Haumea Incident stabbing at her.

"Open the comms channel," the captain ordered.

"Please...help us." A harried man's voice came over the distorted comm line. "...can't hold out much...thirty-seven crew onboard...we are..."

Suddenly, a huge explosion of light flared in the distance.

Eve's shoulders sagged. The cargo ship was gone.

"Goddammit," the XO bit out.

The front legs of the larger Kantos ship in front of them started to glow orange.

"They're going to fire," Eve said.

The captain straightened. "Evasive maneuvers."

His crew raced to obey the orders, the *Polaris* veering suddenly to the right.

"The swarm ships will be on their way back." Eve knew the Kantos loved to swarm like locusts.

"Release the tridents," the captain said.

Good. Eve watched the small, triple-pronged space mines rain out the side of the ship. They'd be a dangerous minefield for the Kantos swarm.

The main Kantos ship swung around.

"They're locking weapons," someone shouted.

Eve fought the need to shout out orders and offer the captain advice. Last time she'd done that, she'd ended up in shackles.

The blast hit the *Polaris*, the shields lighting up from the impact. The ship shuddered.

"Shields holding, but depleting," another crew member called out.

"Sub-Captain Traynor?" The captain's dark gaze met hers.

Something loosened in her chest. "It's a raider-class cruiser, Captain. You're smaller and more maneuverable. You need to circle around it, spray it with laser fire. Its weak spots are on the sides. Sustained laser fire will eventually tear it open. You also need to avoid the legs."

"Fly circles around it?" a young man at a console said. "That's crazy."

Eve eyed the lead pilot. "You up for this?"

The man swallowed. "I don't think I can..."

"Sure you can, if you want us to survive this."

"Walker, do it," the captain barked.

The pilot pulled in a breath and the *Polaris* surged forward. They rounded the Kantos ship. Up close, the bronze-brown hull looked just like the carapace of an insect. One of the legs swung up, but Walker had quick reflexes.

"Fire," Eve said.

The weapons officer started firing. Laser fire hit the Kantos ship in a pretty row of orange.

"Keep going," Eve urged.

They circled the ship, firing non-stop.

Eve crossed her arms over her chest. Everything in her was still, but alive, filled with energy. She'd always known she was born to stand on the bridge of a starship.

"More," she urged. "Keep firing."

"Swarm ships incoming," a crew member yelled.

"Hold," Eve said calmly. "Trust the mines." She eyed the perspiring weapons officer. "What's your name, Lieutenant?"

"Law, ma'am. Lieutenant Miriam Law."

"You're doing fine, Law. Ignore the swarm ships and keep firing on the cruiser."

The swarm ships rushed closer, then hit the field of mines. Eve saw the explosions, like brightly colored pops of fireworks.

The lasers kept cutting into the hull of the larger Kantos ship. She watched the ship's engines fire. They were going to try and make a run for it.

"Bring us around, Walker. Fire everything you have, Law."

They swung around to face the side of the Kantos ship straight on. The laser ripped into the hull.

There was a blinding flash of light, and startled exclamations filled the bridge. She squinted until the light faded away.

On the screen, the Kantos ship broke up into pieces.

Captain Chen released a breath. "Thank you, Sub-Captain."

Eve inclined her head. She glanced at the silent crew. "Good flying, Walker. And excellent shooting, Law."

But she looked back at the screen, at the debris hanging in space and the last of the swarm ships retreating.

They'd keep coming. No matter what. It was ingrained in the Kantos to destroy.

They had to be stopped.

Eon Warriors

Edge of Eon
Touch of Eon
Heart of Eon
Also Available as Audiobooks!

PREVIEW: GLADIATOR

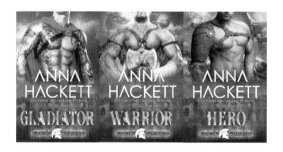

F ighting for love, honor, and freedom on the galaxy's lawless outer rim...

When Earth space marine Harper Adams finds herself abducted by alien slavers off a space station, her life turns into a battle for survival. Dumped into an arena on a desert planet on the outer rim, she finds herself face to face with a big, tattooed alien gladiator...the champion of the Kor Magna Arena.

A former prince abandoned to the arena as a teen, Raiden Tiago has long ago earned his freedom. Now he

195

rules the arena, but he doesn't fight for the glory, but instead for his own dark purpose--revenge against the Thraxian aliens who destroyed his planet. Then his existence is rocked by one small, fierce female fighter from an unknown planet called Earth.

Harper is determined to find a way home, but when she spots her best friend in the arena--a slave of the evil Thraxian aliens--she'll do anything to save her friend...even join forces with the tough alpha male who sets her body on fire. But as Harper and Raiden step foot onto the blood-soaked sands of the arena, Harper worries that Raiden has his own dangerous agenda...

Galactic Gladiators
Gladiator
Warrior
Hero
Protector
Champion
Barbarian
Beast
Rogue
Guardian
Cyborg
Imperator
Also Available as Audiobooks!

Touch of Eon

Heart of Eon

Also Available as Audiobooks!

Galactic Gladiators

Gladiator

Warrior

Hero

Protector

Champion

Barbarian

Beast

Rogue

Guardian

Cyborg

Imperator

Also Available as Audiobooks!

Hell Squad

Marcus

Cruz

Gabe

Reed

Roth

Noah

Shaw

Holmes

Niko

Finn

Theron

Hemi

Ash

Levi

Manu

Griff

Also Available as Audiobooks!

The Anomaly Series

Time Thief

Mind Raider

Soul Stealer

Salvation

Anomaly Series Box Set

The Phoenix Adventures

Among Galactic Ruins

At Star's End

In the Devil's Nebula

On a Rogue Planet

Beneath a Trojan Moon

Beyond Galaxy's Edge

On a Cyborg Planet

Return to Dark Earth

On a Barbarian World

Lost in Barbarian Space

Through Uncharted Space

Crashed on an Ice World

Perma Series

Winter Fusion

A Galactic Holiday

Warriors of the Wind

Tempest

Storm & Seduction

Fury & Darkness

Standalone Titles

Savage Dragon

Hunter's Surrender

One Night with the Wolf

For more information visit AnnaHackettBooks.com

ABOUT THE AUTHOR

I'm a USA Today bestselling author and I'm passionate about ***action romance***. I love stories that combine the thrill of falling in love with the excitement of action, danger and adventure. I'm a sucker for that moment when the team is walking in slow motion, shoulder-to-shoulder heading off into battle. I write about people overcoming unbeatable odds and achieving seemingly impossible goals. I like to believe it's possible for all of us to do the same.

My books are mixture of action, adventure and sexy romance and they're recommended for anyone who enjoys fast-paced stories where the boy wins the girl at the end (or sometimes the girl wins the boy!)

For release dates, action romance info, free books, and other fun stuff, sign up for the latest news here:

Website: www.annahackettbooks.com

25015990R00123

Printed in Great Britain
by Amazon